C000084811

'*Staying On* is a trademark sweet-and-sour Mike Leigh film in novel form and a fictional re-tread of Joe Cawley's *More Ketchup than Salsa*. Updating both to our worrying post-Brexit times where the shifting of boundaries forces us to question where we truly feel we belong'

Matthew Hirtes, author of *Going Local in Gran Canaria*

'A timely tale… I raced through this warm-hearted, warts-and-all portrayal of a broken family, its members fighting to love one another while haunted by the past and afraid of what the future holds. Funny and thought-provoking, *Staying On* is an ideal summer read.'

S.D. Robertson author of *Time to Say Goodbye*

'Beautifully written by an author who's obviously a keen observer of people… a book I admired… I suspect that many people will love it'

Bookbag

STAYING ON

STAYING ON

C.M. TAYLOR

DUCKWORTH

First published in the United Kingdom by Duckworth in 2018

Duckworth, an imprint of Prelude Books Ltd
13 Carrington Road, Richmond,
TW10 5AA, United Kingdom
www.preludebooks.co.uk

For bulk and special sales please contact
info@preludebooks.co.uk

A catalogue record for this book is available
from the British Library

Typeset by Danny Lyle
DanJLyle@gmail.com

Printed in the UK by Clays Ltd

ISBN 978-0-7156-5337-1

1 3 5 7 9 10 8 6 4 2

for my Mum, Mary Taylor, Treeton Stretch

Champion, 1957-58

CONTENTS

APART

TONY

When they'd first moved out to Spain at the end of the last century it was freedom for Tony and Laney Metcalfe, it was the longest summer ever, it was spread your bloody wings and fly after all those years in wet old England, slaving away, chucking any extra in the pension and praying Tony's heart didn't give up before they cashed out and ran. The dream they'd shared with thousands of other post-war babies came true, they'd downed tools for good and pitched up to the sunshine villas of the Costas and the valleys.

God, it was cracking, a true adventure for folks who'd never had one, folks who'd clocked on to work aged fifteen and not drawn breath since…

Getting half-cut at some rustic taverna then strolling back full of *tapas*, moving slowly through the groves, orange blossom sparkling up the air, the sweet must of the pines coming off the hills. Then another glass of *tinto* and skinny-dipping in the pool beneath Orion. No narky boss to get up for. No mortgage to scramble to pay. Needy kids all grown-up a thousand bloody miles off.

Paradise in the mountains – until the arse fell out of things in 2008.

The banks went mad and the worth of the villas nosedived and the pension pots shrunk and inflation took its toll. Tony and Laney's friends started moving back to England.

Dale and Debs with the big hair, they'd gone back first. Then Darren and Jen with dogs, and that German couple who did the swinging. The Dutchies had gone too, a few of them, which had played havoc with the darts league. The Northern Europeans were leaving thes.

And it wasn't just because of money. As the pension tribes of the happy valleys got older, they started to think what it would be like to die out in Spain, or to be widowed and left all alone. Especially when Maureen's husband Walter pegged out while eating a toastie in front of *Match of the Day*, leaving Maureen marooned and grieving in a land which suddenly seemed more foreign than it ever had before.

For a while it had got so that everyone had either gone home or was arguing between themselves about going home. Not that Tony had said anything to Laney about going back. He'd got more chance of crapping in the Queen's handbag than he had of getting his Laney back to England.

So they'd stayed on, and it had calmed down after the first wave of expats had returned. But now this bastard Brexit had come on the scene and stirred things up again.

Tony looked at the English tabloids strewn across his bar. Brexit bloody this; Brexit bloody that.

Britain was leaving the EU, if they'd ever bloody get on with it.

Straight after the vote, it had looked like the expats might get kicked out of Spain, that the EU would send the UK lot packing, and of course the other way round. But now, after throats had been cleared and statements made and lunches devoured in London and in Brussels, it seemed chances were growing that everyone could stay where they were. There might be some forms to fill and some hoops to jump, but the threat of being booted out was fading.

The first Brexit threat had passed, yes, but the questions it asked still remained.

In those first days of uncertainty, every expat in the village had been in conclave: harried, anxious, talking. What where they going to do? Go back? Stay on?

Where exactly was home?

The question still hung over the village. And there were thousands more expats right across Spain asking the same question. And thousands more in Portugal, in Greece and France. Just as there were thousands of Europeans having the same thoughts about Britain. People were jumbled up and worried, everyone was puzzled about home.

But whatever Tony felt, he knew Laney wouldn't go back; she'd find some bear cave up in the hills and hide out for years if she had to, defending herself with a hair clip and spoon. She'd never set foot in England again.

Tony lifted a couple of wine bottles up by their necks – one red, one white – and plonked them on the bar. He got some glasses out then set to work opening the bottles, watching Laney come in from the kitchen carrying a big platter of food.

'Queen of the sarnies,' said Tony.

Laney slid the platter down onto the table that they'd laid for lunch in the middle of their pub – four chairs waiting around it, a slim vase of wild valley flowers speckling cheerfully in the centre. Not that the table was laid for a cheerful reason. They were about to have the Last Supper, their version of it at least. Tony and Laney were laying on a lunch in Viva España to say goodbye to Keith and Pam, two of their oldest expat mates. Keith and Pam were going home. Straight after the vote they'd decided to get out, and they'd not seemed likely to change their minds since.

Brexit had done it for Keith and Pam; Brexit had sent them packing.

But Tony and Laney were staying on.

Laney turned and walked back the way she'd come.

Tony listened to her clatter-bang in the kitchen. Tidying up, she called it. By which she meant putting all the dirty things in a pile for him to do later.

He looked around the empty pub.

He'd cleaned it that morning. Hangover or not, he'd been up at six while Laney slept. And it looked okay. Or maybe he was just used to it, used to the nautical things strung everywhere, the frayed fishing nets and plastic lobsters on the wall, the oars hanging from the ceiling, the telescope and compass over the bar. When they'd first put it up he'd thought it was weird, what with Viva being up in the mountains, nowhere near the sea.

They'd got it all – *memorabilia*, they'd called it, *nautical memorabilia* – from some other expat place closing down on the coast. It was going free and Laney liked the idea of a theme for their bar. Laney said it was 'a theme'.

They'd festooned Viva with the nautical objects, made it into some unlikely shipyard way up in the hills, and it'd been there so long now that it seemed normal and okay to Tony.

The front door rattled. 'Monsieur,' a voice boomed from the doorway.

Tony glanced over. It was Keith in his football top, pretending to be French. Keith often pretended to be French, even though they were in Spain. Tony had just run with it, never asked Keith why. Pam followed in behind Keith. Pam had had her hair done. She was grinning, chuffed probably about finally getting her way and going home to England.

'Tony,' Pam said.

Tony nodded and Pam disappeared into the kitchen to speak to Laney. Keith approached the bar. He flipped through a pile of old English tabloids, looking for the remote control which he palmed up then zapped at the TV in the corner. 'Have you heard what's happening now?'

Tony hadn't heard. He poured the drinks. White for Keith and Laney; red for him and Pam. The TV woke up. There was some English politician on the Spanish rolling news who hadn't been seen since the 1980s. But somehow he'd found a camera crew and he was rattling on about the Falklands War. He was saying, more or less, that if Spain used Brexit as a pretext to try and take back Gibraltar then they could expect gunships in the Med, just like the Argies got up them when they tried to swipe the Falklands.

Tony squinted. What was this politician lad on about?

'What a closet,' said Keith. 'Pouring merde into a pot he'll never have to eat from.'

'Right,' said Tony. He didn't want to know. History was gathering all around him and it could crush him in its grasp. He'd rather not think about it. Tony whipped the remote from Keith's hand, aimed it at the TV, shut down the loopy British throwback. He put the drinks on a tray.

'Big day then,' said Tony.

'The removal people are loading up le stuff now.'

'You can stay with us tonight, Keith.'

'I know, merci.'

'You can though.'

'L'hotel's booked.'

'You can unbook it.'

'I know, thanks. Just want a quiet nuit.'

'You can have a quiet nuit with us, Keith.'

'I know but l'hotel's booked.'

'Suit yourself,' said Tony, topping Keith up.

Tony walked round from behind the bar with the drinks on a tray and put them carefully on the table. Pam and Laney came out of the kitchen and sat down. Keith and Tony sat down too.

'Cheers,' they all said, and started boozing.

'You can stay with us tonight, you know,' said Laney.

'Their l'hotel's booked,' said Tony.

'Not you as well,' said Pam.

'L'afraid so,' said Tony.

'What time's your flight?' asked Laney.

'Dead early tomorrow matin,' said Keith. 'Got to do the airport run in the middle of the bloody night.'

'I'll take you,' said Tony. And he would even, though he was a pensioner and it'd kill him to see his mates go, he'd still get up at the crack to help them out.

'We've booked a taxi,' said Pam. 'Thanks all the same.'

'Good riddance,' said Laney. 'Tuck in.'

'Ooh la la,' said Keith, biting his sarnie.

'Everything sorted then?' asked Laney.

'Hardly,' said Pam. 'Not had a single nibble on the villa.'

'Can you do le pool, Tony, while…' Keith started, until Tony cut him off with his eyes.

The thing with the swimming pools was a secret from Laney. He didn't want to scare her about how bad things were.

Tony dived in, changed the subject. 'You can get home all right, can you?' he asked.

'Course they bloody can,' said Laney. 'They're not geriatrics.'

'We are actually,' said Pam.

'I mean, you can afford a place in England?' asked Tony. 'Even though you haven't sold?'

'Just,' said Keith. 'Only just. It's tight as l'arseholes.'

'Tiny place,' said Pam.

'Cosy,' said Tony.

'On the sea. A flat. Scarborough.'

'Oh, Scarborough,' said Tony.

'Have you been?' asked Pam.

'Only a hundred bloody times,' said Laney.

'Best cricket ground in the county,' remembered Tony. 'Best fish and chips.'

'Here we go,' said Laney. 'Memory Lane.'

'You could come back too,' Pam said.

'Sarnie?' Laney picked up the plate, wafted it around.

'You could though.' Pam tried again. 'You've seen what happens when you stay out here. One of you gets ill… I want to be buried in a little churchyard at home. Not in some dusty plot with a bloody cactus growing over me head.'

Laney was fidgeting at her serviette. She ripped it, her chair grated as she stood and marched back to the kitchen.

'Well done, Pam,' said Keith. 'You numpty.'

'What?' said Pam.

'You're as sensitive as a bloody rock.'

'What? What have I done?' Pam shot Keith a glare. She stood up. She followed Laney in.

'You could come back,' Tony heard Pam say.

'I can't,' said Laney. 'Never.'

Laney stepped away and opened the fridge. 'We've got trifle.'

'Trifle,' Keith said to Tony. 'Magnifique.'

'The Trifle Tower,' said Tony absently, eyes narrowed on Laney in the kitchen.

'Le Tour Trifle,' said Keith.

It was night time. Tony was all in. He was propped up in bed on pillows.

It was daft – he was nearly seventy but he still hadn't worked out how to get comfy. He shuffled around but it didn't help. He had another wriggle. He was grumpy as a pig in nettles.

Tony picked the remote control up off the bedside table, aimed it at the little bedroom set.

Flick, flick, flick, he went up the channels.

Flick, flick, flick, he went back down.

'Found anything?' Laney shouted through from the titchy en-suite bathroom.

'Have I chuff,' Tony said. 'There's nothing on.'

He heard a little tinkle as she took her earrings out, put them on the glass shelf above the en-suite sink. 'I checked tomorrow's weather,' Laney said. 'Boiling here again tomorrow. Pissing it down in England.'

Laney was happy about that. She loved it when the weather was crap back home in England, or when there were twenty-mile traffic jams, or when someone had to pay four million quid for a garage, or a tenner for a loaf of bread.

'Absolutely pissing it down over there,' she said. 'All bloody day.'

Tony thought of the rain falling on the churchyard in their old village, thought of the rain drenching the roof of their old house.

'Come on Tony, what we watching?'

Tony had another flick. There was bugger all on. Well there was, but Tony had seen most of it, and anyway it had nothing much to do with him, not the way he was feeling. He *did* want to watch a film, but whenever he read the little text summary that told you about it, he got upset somehow. Take this film here, some American film about a lad, some shy teenage lad who went away from home for the summer, met a lass, lost his cherry, realised his step-dad was a pillock and that the world was a big place, then after the summer came home all manly.

A *coming of age* story, they called it in the information blurb.

But so what? Tony had come of age long ago.

He elbowed at his pillows. He huffed and he grumbled.

Then take this next film – Tony got the blurb up – about a man who'd had his own coming of age summer many years before, but now was in his early forties, drunk, bitter, worried that he'd taken the wrong path in life, that all his dreams had slipped away.

A *mid-life crisis* story, they called that.

But Tony was well beyond his mid-life.

He knew he wasn't exactly an A-lister, was hardly a man of wild interest to the wider world, but tonight Tony didn't want a story about a boy becoming a man, or about a middle-aged moper straightening things up. Tony wanted a story about a grumpy bastard, a clapped-out working man, hundreds of miles from home, thinking of the rain falling on his old house's roof – a codger past his pension date who still couldn't get comfy in his own chuffing bed. The crap sort of bloke that doesn't usually get a story. He wanted someone to give him that.

'Bugger,' said Tony. 'Balls.'

He pulled the pillow out from behind him, and lobbed it down on the floor, so as to punish it for its stodginess.

'You all right?' Laney shouted in from the en-suite. 'I'm nearly done.'

Bollocks to this, Tony thought.

He wanted to shout, but he didn't. Tony never shouted anything. Apart from in his head.

He flicked the bed clothes off, slid his feet into his slippers, padded out from the bedroom into the hall of the little villa. He moved into the lounge. He slumped down on the worn couch, looked round. Everything seemed as it always did – the big TV, the wine rack stacked with cheap plonk, the glitzy photo frames in their little alcove. Photos of their grown-up son Nick who'd gone off to university and swallowed a thesaurus and bagged himself a posh girl. Photos of their three-year-old grandson Fred, shiny as a boiled sweet. Photos of all the family.

He felt knackered suddenly. He pinched his temples. He slumped and sighed. Was he going to cry? He'd been doing that a bit of late.

Tony looked round the room, like he'd done a thousand times before. He could barely see it, he'd seen it so often. He knew at his age he was expected to be some locked box that stayed the bloody same, that sat there getting crap socks for Christmas and eating butties and watching TV and getting pissed, letting the doctors find new words to describe the bits falling off him, occasionally spilling on his cardigan.

But Tony wanted more than that. Was wanting to change things that had gone wrong in life too much to ask? He looked round the tired old lounge. Was growing old the only growing left?

'Tony,' Laney called out from the bedroom. 'Where are you, you daft bat?'

He didn't reply.

'You in one of your trances?'

He looked at the wall.

'That Bruce Willis film you like's on again.'

But Tony didn't like Bruce Willis. It was Laney that bloody did. He lay down on the sofa and had a wriggle. He couldn't get comfy anywhere.

He must have dozed off on the sofa but he sat bolt upright when the phone rang in the night. Sleep fell off him quicker than water. His heart was unruly with the sound of the ringing. A landline going off after 10pm was never good news.

He swung his legs quickly onto the cool stone floor and stared at the phone on the little rattan table across the room. It was Nick calling, Tony knew it. Something had happened to his son Nick, or else to his grandson Fred. It was awful. The phone ringing was like a bell tolling.

Laney appeared anxious in the doorway. She glanced at Tony, her face pinched and pale.

'Get it then,' said Laney.

'I am,' said Tony.

He stood, moved groggily over, paused, lifted the receiver.

'Hello,' said Tony, then he listened.

'Right,' he said. 'Right. Of course. Twenty minutes.'

When Tony put the phone down he turned to Laney.

'What?' she said. 'What?'

'Keith and Pam's taxi's not shown. They can't get another in time.'

So in the middle of the night Tony drove for hours to put his best mate Keith on a plane that he wished he was taking himself, then he drove back home alone and he climbed exhausted into bed and he lay awake and cried on his own.

It was Tony's seventieth birthday but it wasn't exactly a party.

He was sat on his patio by the pool. He looked around him. Keith and Pam weren't there, and none of the others who'd moved back to England before were there either. Time was, the patio would have been rammed with boozers. Dale would be pretending a breadstick was his moustache. Maureen would be telling that story about her nephew and the binman. Not now though. They were all gone.

Laddo and Shirl were the only ones left. They were over for pre-dinner drinks.

Clumsy Laddo had just knocked a full glass of wine over Tony.

'Sorry, Tony,' said Laddo, cringing behind his big glasses.

Tony looked down at his shirt. It was a birthday present from his wife Laney. There was a wine stain spreading across it. Tony was upset. More than the spill on the shirt allowed. He looked over to Laney. She had her big shades on and some white linen shawly thing turbaned round her head. She was tanned, Laney, always. Bronze as a statue, and still as one too. Because Laney just sat silent on the patio, face in the evening sun, drinking it in like some mad Cleopatra.

He looked at Laney but she didn't look back. She wasn't going to help him.

'Give us a minute,' he said.

Tony walked inside, through the sun lounge and into the kitchen, the ceiling fan chopping round above him. He dabbed at his birthday shirt with a cloth. It was too smart for his tastes. Too swish. Them polo shirts you got in Lidl would do him. Three for eight quid, well eight Euros, which was near enough quids these days – bastard bloody Brexit having shafted sterling.

He'd just pop a polo shirt on. He breathed deep, worried at his teeth. He was whittling about his son Nick. Tony had had a few pairs of socks sent over from England from Nick, but as yet he'd had no call. Not even a call on the big seven-o. Probably having one of his bad days, Nick. Tony went to the bedroom, chose a navy polo, popped that on. Then he heard it. A clear peel of laughter from outside. It was Laney, killing herself laughing at something Shirl or Laddo had said. God he loved her laugh. It was just like Nick's, rare to show but then jagged and leaping like some mad bird's song chucked out from her gut. It was a brilliant laugh.

Tony stepped outside. 'We off then?'

They were going to eat at Pepe's. Tony wasn't overjoyed about that, what with things as they were, but there was no other place to eat in the village, and he couldn't very well eat at his own pub on his birthday, so Tony had shut Viva for the night.

'Come on,' he said.

'Not just yet,' said Shirl, reaching down into her bag. 'Got you something.'

Tony was pleased. He wouldn't have said anything if they hadn't, but he was glad there was a present.

Shirl started to hand the present over, but, 'Hang on, hang on,' said Laddo. 'Little speech.'

'Oh Christ,' said Shirl.

Laddo paused, twitched a little. 'In the years, Tony,' Laddo began, sliding his big glasses back up his nose, 'since you sold up and moved to the valley, what has been our main topic of conversation?'

'Bastard football,' said Laney, breaking from her sunbathing trance.

'Yes, we have discussed football,' Laddo said. 'With Tony here showing he knows utterly bollock all about it.'

Tony looked at Laddo. He was standing up now, like he was giving a speech at a wedding. 'The thing that Tony always bangs on about...'

'Me,' the bronze Laney statue said.

'Apart from you, Laney.'

'Prices,' the statue managed. 'He's always moaning about prices.'

Tony flinched and took a swig of his wine. 'Not as much as Laddo,' he said.

'Who's counting?' asked Laney.

I am, thought Tony, *every bloody penny.*

'The thing Tony always bangs on about is Yorkshire.'

Do I? thought Tony.

'God's country,' murmured Laney.

'It's all *sticklebacks* and *tarns* and *ginnels*, and *when I were a lad*,' continued Laddo.

Shirl laughed. Laney had a little smile.

Tony was sweating now. He had a scratch of his chin.

'Though actually God knows why Tony misses England.' Laddo shoved his glasses right up his nose. 'They laugh at us expats back in England. Spain is for thickies and lowlife. And they all go off to Italy, don't they, like in that old film, *A Room with a View*. They stay in some Tuscan hill town, creaming themselves about pasta and *palazios*.'

'Laddo's been brooding,' explained Shirl. 'Very intense of late.'

'Now if we were round a pool tonking booze just like this in bastard Tuscany, rather than here on the Costa Blanca, oh, they'd be writing books about our exquisite lives, about our fine experiences, but here we're a bunch of chavs on the piss. Nobody wants our story. We're not *aspirational* are we?'

'Bravo!' said Laney.

But Laddo hadn't finished. 'How can you miss it, Tony? How can your home be where you're not welcome? How can you go where they're ashamed to have you?'

Tony looked up to see the sun going down behind the mountains. What was Laddo saying? Was he right? His heart felt empty and sad. Laddo couldn't be right. England wasn't ashamed of him. It *couldn't* be. He thought of his own dad. When he'd come back from the war they'd built hospitals and schools and houses to thank the working people, and the government ran the trains and the gas and later the phones, and hard work and sweat was what got you on. People couldn't have forgotten that. England was cricket and creaky pubs and fish and chips – a trout in a mill stream; a cottage bronzed by an August dusk. That was England, not shame and spite and snobbery.

When Tony looked back, Laddo was looking right at him. 'Tony thinks that home is a place, rather than the people you love.'

'Finished?' Shirl asked Laddo. 'So anyway, Tony, we got you this.'

Shirl handed over a present. It was like a little tube, all wrapped up and Tony shook off his strange mood and took it gratefully and wedged his thumb in beneath the sticky tape, gave it a yank. There was a newspaper inside which Tony unfurled.

'*Yorkshire Evening Post*,' said Tony. 'Brilliant. A subscription.'

'A *copy*,' said Laddo.

'Oh, right. From the day he was born or something,' said Laney.

'No. It's last week's,' said Laddo.

Right. So his present was last week's copy of a newspaper he read on his computer for free.

'Yeah, we just saw it lying round in a pub in Benidorm. Just slipped it into Shirl's bag.'

'Yeah,' said Shirl. 'Soon as we saw it we thought of you and took it.'

Tony looked at Laddo and Shirl; they were both looking at him, smiling. They didn't want him to say thanks again, did they?

'Thanks,' Tony said, ever compliant.

*

They stepped onto the track at dusk and walked slowly through the groves; the olive trunks were squat and gnarled, matt leaves splashed beneath with a soft grey silver and the air spangled with scents: a pocket of clean almond, a spicy swarm of orange blossom. Beside the dusty path they passed a tethered donkey scratching its neck against a crumbling wall; behind them a goat bell clanged flatly from the hills. They walked by fig trees, early summer fruit still pimply and green, broad green leaves like squashed hands. An old man in a darned purple jumper tended his pumpkins.

'It's better than a brochure,' Laney said.

'No refunds,' said Shirl. 'No cancellations.'

Venus was above them. The sky was a made-up blue. They could see the village now, thin streets rising smoothly up a soft dome, a hill like half an eggshell. Tony took Laney's hand.

'The Tit will be lively tonight,' Laddo called back.

Laddo had named their village The Tit because it was on a pert hill.

He called the church in the square at the top of the village The Nip.

Laddo and Shirl, along with Tony and Laney and a few other expats – the ones who were left – lived out of the village, in an expat urbanisation built in the 1970s. The urbanisation was a little group of houses just below The Tit, in a little hollow. Laddo had a name for that too.

'Pepe's will be busy,' said Laney.

Pepe's success made Tony anxious. He dropped Laney's hand. She didn't notice; she was looking at the village ahead of them. 'I could just eat the bloody place,' she said. 'Paradise in the mountains.'

'Long way from Yorkshire, kid,' called back Laddo, cuddling Shirl ahead.

They made the slope of the village's hill, walked up by the stone bodega, up through the thin streets with their shuttered houses, up past the half-finished flats, just concrete and steel since they stopped work in 2008 after the banks had gone mad, and somehow work had just never started again. Slowly they passed the ironmongers, a villager in a vest welding a latch onto a gate, a cat hiding in a shady stone bowl. Their feet were getting heavy. They were nearly at the top. Laddo and Shirl passed the bakery and a girl spilled out, the baker's lass, clattering almost into Tony. The girl smiled up at him, chattering away like mad in Spanish, explaining something to Tony.

'No hablo español,' Tony said apologetically.

Across the street, the widow who ran the tobacconist's muttered, '*Brexit idiota Inglés*,' then slammed her shutter closed. Tony flinched. The baker's girl ran off, gliding into some village alley to disappear.

They came up into the village square, the white-washed church on one side, a stone drinking fountain shaded by a honeysuckle trellis in the centre. It was cool and quiet beneath the trellis and when Laney and Tony had first come to the village, they'd sat beneath the honeysuckle, used it as a sunshade. They'd been dazzled by the square, at least Laney had.

Tony remembered it exactly. He'd put his water bottle under the fountain and twisted the little tap on, then turned to listen to Laney. 'We could though, Tony,' she'd said. 'We could run a little pub-cafe thing, make it work.' Tony had turned back to the fountain. The tap was dry. His water bottle was still empty. 'You can't go on with your job Tony. We could get a little business.'

That was fifteen years ago. And still the fountain ran dry.

Back at Tony's birthday night out, Laddo was ahead, singing some daft song. The baker's girl who'd gabbled at Tony ran into the square and looked at him. '*Por favor, por favor*,' the kid shouted, pointing. The baker's kid turned around and slapped her bum at the expats, belting off down another street.

'I blame the parents,' said Laddo.

'I wish I knew what she said,' said Tony.

'She said you were an arse,' said Laney.

I am an arse, Tony thought sadly. *A massive arse. A great big slab of Yorkshire arse.*

He didn't want to look over but he had to. Tony's own pub, Viva España, stood closed beyond the fountain on the far side of the square next to the church. It was dark and quiet inside Viva and outside a string of unlit bulbs sagged across the façade, empty plastic tables slung out on the tarmac beneath them.

Laney steered Tony over towards Pepe's on the other side of the square. People were spilling out of Pepe's, drinking and chatting in small groups across the pavement and even into the square. But it wasn't just busy outside: as they neared – Laddo and Shirl ahead – they heard the buzz from inside.

'Good job we booked,' said Laddo, holding the door open.

Laddo shoved his big glasses up his nose, then shouldered inside, leaving a path in the crowd for Shirl, then Laney and Tony, to follow. Laddo led through the bar to the smaller restaurant room by the side. It was quieter. The floor was a creamy marble, the walls were hung with abstract paintings, bright scruffy rectangles standing on top of bright green squares. Stacks of black lines sliced through with white lines. All hand-painted, all original work. Pepe's work. Ten or so canvasses, paintings covering every wall and nowhere a photo or a picture of the valley, nothing to show where you were.

Laddo and Shirl, Tony and Laney, moved into the room.

The table they'd reserved was empty by the window, which was good. But a bloke they couldn't stand – The Font – was sitting in the way and there was no way to avoid him.

'Bit of local food, eh,' said The Font. 'Night off from your chicken in a basket.'

'We sell a lot of that,' said Laney.

They didn't sell a lot of it, Tony thought. *Not enough anyway.*

'I didn't mean anything by it.'

But he did. He had. The Font had meant something by it.

They walked on.

'Try the *arròs negra*,' The Font called after them. 'It's wonderful tonight.'

The Font was called The Font because he acted like he knew everything. He was the font of all knowledge, or so he thought at least. And it was true that The Font did seem to know a lot of things, especially about Spain. More than they did anyway. Because The Font was 'integrated' – that's what he called it. He lived in the village, not in the urbanisation, along with almost all of the other incomers. And he didn't just speak 'restaurant Spanish' like the rest. Font was even on the village council.

Tony, Laney, Shirl and Laddo took their table by the window. Tony stared through the window towards his dark, quiet pub.

Then Pepe was stood by the table in an ironed white shirt. He had a mark on his shirt. Not a wine stain like Tony had had, but paint. A drip of dark green paint on his collar. Nobody said anything. Practically all Pepe's clothes had paint splodges on them. He was holding four menus which he handed out.

'And one for the birthday boy,' said Pepe.

They didn't even bother trying to talk to Pepe in Spanish anymore. They had tried once or twice, when they'd first come, when they were still trying to learn the language, but at some point early on they'd get stuck and Pepe would say 'in English,' and they'd switch. It'd been like that all over really, at the market, the doctor's, the pharmacy, starting out with stuttering good intentions but then failing quite quickly to get the hang of things, and falling back harder into home: going to Open All Hours not the *supermercado*, reading the English papers, watching the telly – *Strictly, Emmerdale, Come Dine with Me* – Paxo stuffing, Mr Kipling's, a Sunday roast in the sweltering heat. They'd made a shy little leap to try and get hold of Spain but they'd missed and they'd not tried so hard again, instead making themselves comfy in some fond dot-to-dot map they'd drawn of home. It was make do and mend. It was the expat Blitz, and just as with their pub Viva España, their life was Spanish in name alone.

Tony was still looking out the window. He watched a couple of tourists wander by his dark pub and down the little snicket that separated Viva from the church.

'Tony, my friend,' said Pepe.

Tony turned in to face the room. 'Hi, Pepe,' he said.

'You are magnificent, Tony. You are the most exciting man I have seen all year.'

Tony smiled. 'Yep,' said Tony. 'No surprise to me that you say that.'

Tony liked Pepe. He thought he shouldn't because in one way they were rivals, but he did. Pepe was forty-two, around the same age as his own son. It was an odd relationship – sort-of friends but sort-of rivals; in Spain but always in English, like father and son, but not like that either. And talking of fathers... Tony looked around. 'Where's Chico?' he asked.

Old Chico was Pepe's dad. He was usually on a chair by the rubber plant in his carpet slippers, playing cards with himself, watching everything. Chico knew everyone in the bar, knew everything about the village. He never spoke to the expats, never went anywhere, ate all his meals in Pepe's. Chico had about as much chance of leaving the village as a tree did of walking out, so it was a surprise not to see him.

'Where's he gone?'

'Pissed,' said Pepe.

'Chico's pissed,' giggled Shirl.

'Bring us some wine, Pepe, would you?' said Laddo.

'Have whatever you want,' Pepe said with a smile and a nod. 'Everything is on the house.'

'I can't accept that,' said Tony.

'Please, it is your birthday.'

Pepe's nephew came over with a bottle of cava and four glasses. He put them down and started pouring out. Pepe spoke quickly in Spanish to his nephew, then walked away. The seat of his trousers was flecked with violet paint.

Next day, Laney sat on the pub terrace in her shades, a cup smudged with lippy on the table before her. Across the square, Pepe moved around outside his own bar, hosing his window boxes in flip-flops and shorts. Tony was standing outside Viva. He was nursing a coffee and a belting head.

The bloody racket started up again.

Tony frowned towards the broken fountain in the middle of the square. Painful sounds were coming from under the honeysuckle.

He pinched at his temples. The village brass band were practising. They'd met in the square, the band, every Tuesday since the village had lost its hall – 'lost' meaning had it been sold from under them by the regional government to turn into the high-spec flats that lay unfinished to this day.

There were four or five Spanish kids around the broken fountain. Two of the kids – both lasses, dark village girls with thick pelts of hair worn in scruffy mullets, rough-and-tumble sorts – were stood honking on their trumpets, waving their horns this way and that, like they were in some ritzy backing band. The other kids laughed and stood and joined in, the parping tuba and the slide trombone, waggling this way and that. They were having fun. And it might have been fun for Tony too, if he didn't have this poisonous head.

Tony checked his watch against the church's clock.

Five fifty-nine.

The mayor of the village, sleepy old Gabriel, walked into the square with his wife, Consuela with the huge hennaed hair. Consuela with the hair was dressed smartly and was talking quickly on her phone as her husband padded behind her with his trousers tucked inside his socks. Consuela hung up on her call. Neither of them glanced towards Viva, neither of them said hello. Sleepy Gabriel stopped and watched as Consuela walked towards the broken fountain and spoke to one of the two rough-and-tumble band girls – Consuela's daughter, Tony guessed, although he wasn't sure. He only really knew who Gabriel and Consuela were because Pepe told him to vote for Gabriel in the local elections.

As loudly as a goose, Consuela chatted to her daughter. Gabriel stood away from them, marooned in the sunlight, peering suspiciously at the honeysuckle. Tony looked across the terrace to Laney, sitting as still as a statue. Pepe was still quenching his plants. Tony heard the sound of an engine and looked at his watch. The church clock chimed six. A little silver car nipped into the square and Tony waved at Chitta in its driver's seat.

On time every time.

Tony watched Chitta park in the square and climb out. She waved at Pepe and walked towards Viva. Pepe watched her across the square. Laney took off her shades and squinted at Chitta from a half-open eye.

'I didn't know Chitta was due.'

'Just want to check a policy with her.'

Chitta followed Tony into a corner right at the back of Viva, next to the dusty old piano. She got her laptop out and opened up the spreadsheet she'd done for Viva.

They got right down to it. You always did with Chitta.

'These are the figures, Mr Metcalfe, that you asked me to check…'

'It's not that. I…'

'This is the Incoming, here,' said Chitta, running her finger down a column of numbers. 'And this is Outgoing here. Is this what you wanted to see?'

'Yes.'

'Do these figures match your own calculations, Mr Metcalfe?'

'Yes.' They did. Too bloody accurately. He felt hollow inside.

Tony stared at the numbers, looked from the incoming to the outgoing.

'Don't have much in common, do they?' he said.

'If it was just one month, Mr Metcalfe… but they are getting farther apart.'

Tony breathed out hard, grabbed for explanations. 'It's the expats, many going home, the rest tightening their belts.'

'Yes and more will go now, and no more will come now your dipshit country is pretending it's not in Europe. Your happy valley is over,' said Chitta, slapping her laptop shut.

'And the Spanish don't come near me. It's getting worse. *Idiota Brexit.*'

Chitta kept her counsel. Tony's head was banging now. He squinted along the bar-room. Through the window he could see Laney on the terrace. Across the square he could see Pepe, coiling up his hosepipe and heading inside. The village brass band still chatted with Consuela. Gabriel stood sleepy and still. Tony bobbed his head low and leaned towards Chitta. 'What would it fetch?' Tony blurted, not yet realising what he'd said.

'Mr Metcalfe?'

'What would it fetch?' he whispered quickly. 'The pub. What would I get if I sold up to go home?'

Chitta summoned her kindest eyes. 'Nothing.'

'You what! Bollocks. What?'

'You would not find a buyer. Losing money, Mr Metcalfe, with many potential customers going home. Not an attractive proposition.'

'It's a lovely pub.'

'To get rid of this pub and go home, you would first need to make the pub a success.'

Tony went quiet. Chitta slid her laptop into her bag.

'But how? I've tried all sorts. Not so much recently I admit. But you know it's like being a fisherman – if there's not enough fish it doesn't matter how fancy your rod is.'

'There are enough fish,' Chitta said, almost to herself, 'For one fisherman at least.'

'What?'

She checked her watch. Her face went hard. She stood, reached for her bag. Tony's eyes peered sadly up at her. She met them and sighed. 'Look,' she relented. 'There is one way to survive. Maybe. But it us up to you.'

He exhaled. 'Right?'

'I do the accounts for Pepe's.'

He knew that. She'd never said a word before.

'Pepe's fish will not swim home with Brexit,' she said.

Tony squinted down the length of the bar and out across the square. He watched Consuela and Gabriel and all the village band file inside Pepe's.

'You must catch some of Pepe's fish.'

*

Tony was in the kitchen clearing up.

He'd popped the radio on, some golden oldie station playing tea dance music, a rumba he thought. Or maybe a tango. He wasn't up on the names of things, not like Laney who knew them all, although for many years she'd never danced. Tony finished the dishes. He put the sponge and plate down. He took his rubber gloves off and went to find Laney. Didn't take long. She was sitting on the back step, holding a pack of cigarettes. Tony knew she kept a secret stash at the back of the napkin cupboard – a not-so-secret stash, given that he was the only person who ever went in there. Laney was looking at the hills.

Tony watched Laney strike a match then light a cigarette, waving out the flame with a zigzag of her wrist. She pulled deeply on the cigarette, looking at the hills. When Laney breathed out, Tony gagged. He hated the smell. She used it sometimes, he thought, to keep him away from her.

'You know I can't go back,' she said, not turning.

'I never said a word.'

'You didn't have to, Tony Metcalfe.'

The sun was on her hair, making the brown of it russet. If you met her now you might think she was a cow, but Tony knew what she'd been through. She didn't get like this having an easy life. The radio in the kitchen still played. They'd met in 1960 at the bakery in her village. Well, they'd met before but she said she didn't remember. The first time *she* remembered was when she was a Saturday girl at the baker's, wrapping the baps up in brown paper, taking the money, cheeking the customers. Fourteen she was. Tony was sixteen. He'd stopped off on the way to the site he was working on. He'd already paid, his loaf was under his arm, but he'd stayed at the counter. Apart from the two of them the shop was empty. He'd opened his mouth but he didn't speak.

'What?' she'd asked.

Her first words. First word. Fifty-some years ago. She'd told him loads of times since that she'd thought he looked funny, with his hair cut like a granddad's, and his face all gloomy and worried, like he was a grown-up who just happened to be a kid. She said he looked like he'd never even heard the word *teenager*, never been in trouble, like some thrifty war-child always minding his Ps and Qs.

The age gap was only two years but it looked like a valley.

'What?' she said again.

He looked at his boots on the floury wooden floor. 'Come to the dance.'

'No,' Laney said.

'Chips then?'

She didn't say anything to that, and young Tony's hope heard a yes in her silence. After work he was waiting for her outside the baker's.

'You're like a bloody limpet.'

He knew she'd meant to hurt him. It'd worked, but he wouldn't let it show.

'They're frying,' he said.

She turned towards the chipper. They walked up the tiddly main street. The stones of the houses abutting the road were square and black, the cement between them thick and grey. The Bradford bus clattered past them and on through the village. They stopped outside the church and he nodded over the road to the Methodist Hall. They saw a courting couple walk inside, holding hands. He looked down at her hand but he didn't dare touch it. They were only kids.

She nodded towards the chip shop.

Tony patted his granddad's hair. 'Come on then.'

They walked across the road, got vinegary chips with scraps and stood outside, scoffing like a pair of seagulls. Over the road the huge yew tree sheltered the graveyard. From a few doors down, music came softly out from the Methodist Hall. They walked closer. The hall's outer doors were open and the inner doors were glass and inside he could see couples moving around, dancing to the music – *oom cha cha, oom cha cha.*

He watched Laney as she too peered inside.

It was tiny, the movement, so tiny at first that he wasn't sure, but he thought she was swaying. She was; she wanted to dance. She sensed him looking and stopped. She looked away from the hall. But it was too late, he was filled already with courage.

He finished his chips and she finished hers and he took the paper off her and walked across the road, dropping them into the bent iron basket outside the church. He turned to cross back and for a moment they eyed each other across the road. He crossed back and pulled a hanky from his pocket, handing it to her so she could wipe the vinegar from her hands.

Tony turned again to face the hall. 'Come on,' he said.

'I don't like it.'

'Don't be daft... I saw you.'

'What?'

He swayed his body a little, just as he had caught her doing. 'You don't like people looking, do you?'

She didn't deny it. He grew bold.

There was an alley down the side of the Methodist Hall and he took her hand and walked her down it. He knew just where he was going. There was a side door down the alley and Tony guessed it would be open.

He pulled at it. It came. Tony stepped into a small room, a store room, mops and soap and bleach stacked on shelves beside another door. Tony stepped towards that door and opened it slightly. Music from inside the main hall wafted into the store room. Tony looked over to Laney. She was still standing at the entrance, unsure what to do. He reached out his hand.

'Come on. Nobody here but me and thee.'

She looked petrified, but she had a bit of gumption. He'd known that the first time he'd seen her. She stepped towards him, took his hand. He snaffled it up with his own, but then put his other arm lightly on her shoulder, soft as if she was some jumpy cat that was likely to bolt. The music breezed in through the door. The store room was full of clean smells and new smells. They danced.

It was dusk when the music stopped and they stepped back out to the alley. And it was dusk in the valley now. The late sun was still on her hair, shining it up like an apple. The music was still playing in Viva's kitchen. She was still looking out at the hills. He moved up closely behind her.

Sometimes it was like he wasn't even Tony, he was part of Tony and Laney. He'd always loved her more than she'd loved him. He touched her gently and she stood, as though his touch had been a signal. She turned and leaned into him, burrowed close. Sometimes when she was soft, sometimes just for a tiny puff of time, it was like they were courting again. Touching her was like going back in time. The music was still playing in the kitchen in Viva. And the music was still playing in the Methodist Hall back home. He could smell the smells from the store room, as though they were back there now. The past was all around him. Except she was dancing with him in the past, and she would not do that now.

He'd tried everything to fix things up with Laney, but he couldn't because she wasn't honest with herself. The old Laney was in there, he knew it, she just had to face up to things. But he didn't know how to get her to do it.

Tony stared into the water. The heat was mad. Not yet August and it was already a punishment.

Tony picked up the pool brush. He screwed the longest handle to the end of it and dipped it into the cool blue water.

Laney didn't know about this thing with the pools, not really.

When the first expat couple left the valley for home without selling up, Tony had said to them he'd pop round now and then and keep the pool spic and span. Laney knew about that, volunteered him for the job herself. Tony didn't mind. It was helping out.

Then he'd agreed to do the same for the second couple, Roger and Kath. Laney knew about that too. But when the third couple asked, he'd had to start charging money. He didn't want to, but Chitta had made him, said it was taking too much time from the pub.

So now he cleaned seven pools on the urbanisation. Seven pools at twenty quid a month. Hundred and forty quid a month. Not a lot. Especially as it all went straight into the cash register of Viva, on the sly of course, so Laney never caught on how badly the pub was doing.

She couldn't know. He'd never tell how deep it ran. She'd be worried sick. Especially this time of year, as the weeks ticked down to the anniversary. He had to put himself aside and graft. There was no other option.

Every life was full of tight squeezes, full of not gettings and never hads. Everyone lived their lives half-starved inside, didn't they? It was only good manners. You couldn't put yourself first. Life wasn't some gorgeous fruit you could just snatch from the branch. It was a meal that you shared, and someone had to have the grace to not mind being served last. He looked at his watch, looked at the pool.

He had to get this done, he was working in Viva in twenty minutes.

On his way to work in Viva he walked past Pepe's.

There was a noise from inside Pepe's, a bad noise, and Tony looked through the window and saw two figures squaring up in the semi-darkness. One of the figures was Pepe. The other was Lita, a finger jabbing out at her husband, prodding at his chest, her voice a squabble of mardy Spanish. They were having a domestic; another one. Tony started to walk away then stopped; he looked away then looked back. He hated fighting more than anything.

You gave ground, you compromised, you kept the show on the road.

You never made a fuss.

Pepe stood there, took what Lita had to say, then looked down, shook his head, walked away – his silence as much of a curse to Lita as any mouthful he could have given her.

Pepe came clunking out of the darkness towards the front door. He was wearing a waiter's black and whites and had a half-finished canvas under one arm, a wooden box hung over one shoulder, a black shoe splashed with shining silver paint. Tony looked beyond him to Lita, watching her husband walk away, silent now, the gold in her ears and round her neck the only shiny thing about her, her village girl's face sad and pale. She saw Tony and turned away.

Pepe was out of the door now, clutching his kit, his own cheeks pale, his hands shaking. He stood next to Tony in the shadows.

'I need a friend, Tony.'

They walked together through the groves and Pepe stopped and dropped his wooden box down on the dirt between the trees. Pepe rested his half-finished canvas against the wooden box and he flipped the box open and took a bottle of red wine out and tossed it to Tony.

Tony snatched it from the air.

'This wine,' said Pepe, 'I do not sell in the restaurant.'

Tony looked at the murky bottle. He spotted some patchy shade beneath an olive tree and sat down, leaning back against the squat olive trunk. Tony had a swig of wine and watched as Pepe unpacked his wooden box, taking out oil paints and brushes, a knife, jars of water and turps. Pepe pulled out some pieces of folded-up wood which he swung together into an easel. He placed his canvas on the easel and turned back to Tony.

'So?' asked Pepe, nodding towards the bottle.

'Can see why you keep it to yourselves.'

'It's medicine. The village secret.'

'It's why you all live so long.'

'My father, he would not like me sharing with a pale face.'

'Here, take your magic potion back. Don't want to wake the curse of Old Chico.'

'Keep it,' said Pepe. He reached into his box and pulled out a second bottle which he uncorked once more with his teeth.

'Two bottles!' said Tony. 'You drunkard. You didn't know I was coming.'

'My wife is making me very thirsty.'

'You want to talk?'

'I want to paint,' said Pepe, turning his back to Tony and putting down his bottle.

Tony leaned back on the trunk. He drank Old Chico's wine. The valley was hot and quiet. A warm breeze tousled through the groves and Tony looked up to the olive tree above him. The olive leaves were moving, flashing silver in the warm breeze, twitchy and nimble as a school of young fish. And a memory came. He was seven or eight, back home in Yorkshire, he was biking with a pal to a tarn in the village, he was laying down on the bank, wafting a jar in the water to try and catch the darting silver fish.

But he couldn't catch them. He couldn't catch the fish.

Tony looked back to his Spanish friend. Pepe now held a brush. He was working at the canvas with sharp strokes. Tony frowned. He looked from the canvas to the hill, then back to Pepe's canvas. 'I don't understand,' Tony said, peering closely at the canvas: two smudgy orange rectangles, slashed across with green. 'It looks nothing like the hill.'

'I am not painting the hill.'

'Right,' said Tony. 'Or these trees? Or those houses over there?'

'No.'

'What is it then, Pepe?' Tony asked. 'I mean, exactly? If you don't, if you wouldn't mind saying.'

Pepe put down his brush and picked up his father's wine and he stepped closer to Tony. 'Any man,' Pepe said, 'can come to this valley, this paradise in the mountains, and he can paint the sun, the sky, the beautiful trees. It might be a poor painting, but he can do it. Yes?'

Tony nodded.

'This hill. Any person can paint this hill, but I, Tony, I am the only man in the world who can paint my mind.'

'What! Cobblers. Give over,' said Tony, antsy suddenly. 'Christ, man. You've had a row with your wife.' He sat forward. 'That's what you should be sorting. Not worrying about painting your bloody mind.'

Pepe looked hurt. He stepped into the shade and squatted on his haunches. He looked across to Tony. 'You know I was born here?'

'Yes?'

Pepe picked up some earth in his hand. 'So where you were born, Tony, you think that place is beautiful too?'

'I do, yes. As it happens.'

'But you are not there. You and Laney have moved on. But I am still home.'

Tony had a think, had another swig. The penny dropped. 'That's what you and Lita were rowing about.'

'Yes.' Pepe dropped the dirt from his hand. 'My wife will never leave the valley. Her sisters, her mother, her aunts, her business – all are here.' Pepe picked up another handful of dirt, poured it back slowly to the floor. He looked over to the hill without seeing it. 'Her whole life is here Tony. But me, I know I have another life waiting somewhere.'

'Blimey! *Another life waiting*. That's a bit wacky.'

'Just because you are all grown in your body, Tony,' Pepe said, 'it does not mean you must stay the same size in your mind.' Pepe stood and walked back to his canvas. He picked up a paint brush. 'I can change, Tony. You can change too. Although you never will.'

'You what?'

'You do not value your own feelings, Tony.'

Tony sighed and looked away. He'd had enough now.

It was hot and he was drunk, and he was drowsy and heady.

He had a drink and peered around. The breeze came round again, twitching at the olive leaves. He half knew what Pepe was on about, but it all seemed like bluster too. His balls weren't in eggcups. And he could change things if he wanted to, he just didn't want to put himself forward, he didn't want to impose.

Tony was swigging hard at the village wine. He could feel the tears inside his chest. And he could feel that the wine was talking to the tears, but he couldn't hear what either of them were saying.

'Before I spoke to my wife about leaving the valley, Tony, I spoke to our accountant Chitta,' said Pepe, 'about selling Pepe's.'

Beads of sweat were suddenly on his back. 'Oh, right.'

'And you know what she said, Tony?'

'Maybe.'

'She said to get the best price for my bar I must take customers from you.'

'She never. What did you say?'

'I told the truth. I said Viva has not enough customers to take.'

Tony peered in through the window round the back of Pam and Keith's. It was empty. The dining table they'd all sat round – getting pissed, scoffing nibbles, talking bollocks – that was gone.

Pam and Keith were gone. His best mate had left him to die in a foreign field with a failing bar, a morbid wife, and a lifelong case of not standing up for himself. The pressure was building. Something was going to have to give.

Tony put his rucksack down, walked over to the pool house. He leaned in, got the brush, heard a little scuffling sound. He leaned deeper in, moved a tin of paint aside, budged some old tiles. Sat on an old brush head was a bird. A tiny thing.

'Hello, little one.'

He bent right down. His knees clicked.

It moved its wings a little – flew a dainty flight.

'Wings aren't broke then.'

Tony curled a finger, gave the bird – the finch – the gentlest nudge. It skittered off a bit, further into the corner.

'Legs are okay, too.'

Tony puzzled. The bird seemed okay. Why was it stuck there?

He ducked outside, walked to the side of the pool, picked up his rucksack. He pulled out a Tupperware box, opened it, took out a sarnie, ripped off a crust. Then he pulled out his water bottle.

He went back inside. He couldn't see the bird now, it was hiding somewhere, but he knew it was there. He crumbed up the crust, tossed pieces into the corner. Then he found an old jar, pulled off the lid, wiped it clean with his shirt, trickled in some fresh water, put it down.

He backed out, clutching the pool brush and wedging the door ajar so the bird could get out when it wanted.

TOGETHER

LANEY

Laney was certain that Tony was kidding. It just didn't seem likely; it didn't seem right.

'He's never, Tony.'

'He is, Laney. That's what it says here.'

They were at the villa. Tony was pointing at an email on the computer.

'Bloody hell,' said Laney. 'Our Nick.'

'I know.'

'How long's he staying?'

'Doesn't say.'

'Is he hiring a car?'

'Doesn't say. Read the blumming thing yourself, instead of asking me.'

'Bloody hell, our Nick...'

'I know, Laney.'

She felt uncomfortable. She felt suspicious. 'How's he going to pay for it? Thought he was brassick.'

'He's made another record maybe. Do they still have records?' Tony spun round in his chair to face the screen. 'What am I asking you for, Laney. You're not a reliable source. I've got broadband. I can grab the information jugular.'

'You're not having me on are you Tony?'

'It's coming back.'

'What is?'

'Vinyl. Records. Sales are resurgent, it says here. Nick might have made another record. Available across all formats, type-thing. Do you remember how he looked as a kid with that Walkman on?'

Laney was chewing at her nails. 'Him and Jo have finished.'

'I remember one Saturday picking him outside the pool back home and he got in the car and he had them big daft yellow headphones on, that Sport Walkman or something we got him for Crimbo.'

'She's thrown him out. She's not been able to stand his moping.'

'He looked such a closet with those yellow sponge mufflers on his head, and that T-shirt he'd been after for weeks that we had to get him. Lacoste...'

'She was always too good for him.'

'Do you remember that time he just went mad for espadrilles? All he would wear were espadrilles.'

But Laney wasn't listening. 'Jo's shacked up with someone else.'

'No. She's coming too.'

'A barrister, or a doctor with a five-bedroom house.'

'It says here Nick's bringing Jo.'

'What?' Laney stared at the back of Tony's head. 'Never. It can't.'

'It does.' Tony span round in his chair and beamed at Laney. 'She's coming.'

Laney flushed. Bloody hell, Lady Jo in the happy valley. Laney straightened her hair, looked around the room. She felt anxious and hostile. Threatened. Certainly not hospitable. Like a rock had been lobbed into her settled pool. Jo just wasn't like the Metcalfes. Laney looked at Tony, leant forward, straightened his collar. Jo would think Tony was a right bag of muck. Then it hit her. 'What about Fred? Who'll look after the kid? Her lot probably.'

Tony smiled. 'Fred's coming.'

'Never,' said Laney. 'Stop pissing about.'

'He is.'

'He's not.'

'He is.'

'Bloody hell.'

'I know,' said Tony.

'When they coming?'

'Wednesday.'

'Never.'

'Honest.'

'But they've never been out before.'

'Nick has.'

'Hardly.'

'Wonder why they're coming,' said Tony.

'Bloody hell,' said Laney, swigging at her wine. 'Wednesday.'

It was Wednesday.

'If you make me late, Tony Metcalfe, I'll tan your bloody hide.'

'We've got ages, love.'

She eyed the clock on the dashboard. 'It's nearly quarter to.'

'We've got bloody ages.'

Laney knew Tony was right, but that didn't stop her whittling. They were driving to the airport and she wanted to be in there early, poised for when they came through arrivals – not panting in some sweaty mess, a new arrival herself. She knew that Nick and Jo must think she was an old cow for not coming to England since the birth, but she'd show them it wasn't like that, that it was just her condition holding her back.

Laney stared out of the passenger window to the bright hills beyond. She barely saw them. She was gagging for a ciggie. She twisted at her wedding ring, patted her headscarf straight. They weren't in their normal car – it wouldn't easily have fitted Nick, Jo and the lad Fred in, not with their bags. So they'd borrowed Laddo's people wagon or whatever it was called, a seven seater. They'd hired a kiddie seat for it too, for little Fred.

Laney eyed the time. Tony spotted her. 'They've got to go through passports, love. Get their bags.'

'They might only have hand luggage.'

'They've got a bloody kid, Laney. They'll have a bloody mule train. You should see their flat. The absolute crap they've been conned into buying. Mostly Nick, it has to be said.'

'What?'

'The juicers and monitors and medicines and kiddie contraptions they've got piled around that shit hole of a flat.'

'Is it that bad?'

'The flat? Put it this way, Laney love – they are not spic and span.'

'Too posh to clean, is she?'

'Why should she have to do it?' asked Tony. 'Why not Nick? She earns all the bloody brass.'

Laney went quiet.

'Anyway,' Tony said, 'get this. Last time I was over, I asked Jo where they kept the iron.'

'Right. Where was it?'

'You know what she said?'

'What?'

'She said they didn't have one.'

'What?'

'I know.'

'No iron! But…'

'I know. They've got every bloody useless piece of kiddie junk you were ever supposed to have, but they haven't even got an iron.'

'Amazing.'

'Yet they'll buy anything. Nick will. He bought these locks to put on the kitchen drawers so kids can't get into them, and guess what?'

'What?'

'Adults can't get into them either. Well, I can't. Ridiculous.'

'Oh, I don't know, Tony.'

'What?'

'What if little Fred got hold of a knife?'

'Then he'd cut himself and learn a lesson.'

'If he got a second chance.' Laney said. 'You can't be too careful.'

Tony winced and glanced away. He studied the road. There was silence in the car. Laney glanced again at the clock. 'Hurry up, Tony,' she snapped. 'That Jo might be a light packer.'

Laney wouldn't put it past her. A woman without an iron was capable of anything. And she was weird in other ways, Jo, judging from the scraps Laney had gleaned from Tony. Jo was from the village next to theirs in England, from one of them big houses by the park, but she'd moved away when she was young after her parents split up right nastily. Her mum had hit the bottle and her dad had hit her mum, and Jo and her older brother Will had been shunted off to live with an aunt over in some well-to-do part of Cheshire that had a Waitrose.

She acted normal, Jo, but she'd been to university, become a doctor or something. Seemed like a meddler. And why had her and Nick and the lad Fred suddenly come out here, what with it getting close to the anniversary? Laney tilted the car sun-visor down. Jo could bloody whistle for it if she thought she was going to meddle with Laney's family.

Laney looked in the mirror; she stacked her top lip on to her bottom lip and wiggled them together, spreading out her lippy. The Metcalfes were fine; they were doing all right. She popped her lips apart and pouted. Just as well as anybody.

They'd been busy in the last few days. There was a little room with a balcony above Viva; they used it as a store room. But they'd emptied it – it needed doing anyway – given it a paint, stuck a bed in, borrowed a travel cot, made it nice. They'd no idea what Fred was into, but they'd got a kids' magazine, cut some pictures out, stuck them to the wall over his cot. Then they'd been to the *supermercado* and got the things in that Jo and Nick wanted for Fred. Bloody huge list it was too, full of pulses and grains she'd never heard of, and ending with the underlined words, *local and organic wherever possible*. Then they'd got some extra booze in too, lots, because Nick could bloody drink. He'd been thirsty since the moment he'd popped out, Nick, and wouldn't her boobs have known about it if she'd not palmed him off with formula and let him drink his fill.

They pulled off the motorway and onto the airport approach road.

'Finally,' said Laney.

'You'll get to meet the lad then,' said Tony. 'Finally.'

'Stop it.'

'What?'

'Rubbing it in.'

'I'm not, Laney.'

'Just because you've seen him, you big show off.'

'I'm just excited for you.'

'Give over.'

'He's a lovely little thing, Laney. Mouth on him though, like his dad.'

'And his granddad.'

They'd rowed like cats and dogs when Laney had first said she wasn't going over to England for Fred's birth. Tony even swore in anger at her. He had a filthy mouth but it was the first time he'd ever really turned it on her, which had been a surprise, nearly five decades in, to know she'd not quite seen his full repertoire.

Though God knows he'd not seen all of her own.

And anyway, she couldn't go. That's what the doctor said when they'd finally got to the bottom of it. He advised against the trip, which Tony hadn't liked, looking all lonely as he left the house, sad and dapper with his little suitcase. But he went. He found his pluck and got on the plane and went. He got Laney a new mobile phone before he left, made sure he sent her tonnes of pictures. Not that the pictures helped.

Then Tony had gone back to England three more times, once for each of Fred's birthdays. Though there weren't more rows. They were through that fire. Tony just quietly booked his flights, jotted the dates on the calendar, and got Laddo to drive him to the airport. The idea of her going back had been dropped forever. She'd won that fight.

The car stopped. Tony reached out of the driver's window and took a ticket from the bollard. 'Good dog,' he said.

The metal arm in front of them swung up and they drove inside.

'There's one there,' said Laney. 'You missed that one, there's one.'

'Okay, Love,' said Tony. 'Never driven this before. It's a big bugger.'

He was right. She'd shut up. Her heart was banging like anything. 'There we go,' said Tony, sliding into a space.

They got out. She was gagging even more now but she knew she couldn't smoke. She'd stink of it then, and Fred wouldn't come near. Not that he would anyway – he didn't know her, apart from a few goes on Skype. Which was strange because she knew him – the time she'd spent looking at his pictures, cherishing his face, and yet he'd just think she was the fuzzy old bag from Nick's computer. But she wasn't a bag. She smoothed at her shawl, straightened her head scarf. She couldn't be a bag yet. He probably wouldn't kiss her, probably wouldn't cuddle.

They walked away from the car park. Laney had a peek at Tony. He seemed normal, relaxed. It was her that was buckled up, filled with ominous trepidations. She reached out to take his hand. It hurt her that she needed him. It made her angry. He grabbed her hand and squeezed it.

They killed some time with a coffee. They didn't speak. In Arrivals there were other couples – English, retired, waiting for family – and one of the men smiled as they neared the barrier. 'Family sneaking one in before we leave the bloody EU? Last cheap holiday for the grandkids?'

'Won't be cheap for me,' Tony smiled.

Laney stared ahead, all keyed up. She still didn't believe they'd come, really walk through the gate. Nick had been out to the valley a couple of times when they'd first moved out, before he'd met Jo, but he'd not stayed with them long before *ditching the expats* – his words – *and doing some culture in Andalusia*. Laney and Nick had had some pissed row last time he came, she forgot about what. It was nothing. One of them things. Then he'd stopped coming all together – which Tony said was down to her – and Nick'd never brought Jo out to the valley either. Laney had never met her. Despite how hard her and Tony had tried; despite how often they'd dangled the bait. They'd offered holidays with babysitting and the pool, free lifts and grub, a free bar at Viva. Most people would bite your hand off. But they'd never said yes, and they never seemed likely to.

So what had changed now? New arrivals began to trickle through the gate. Laney stared. She twirled the rings on her bronze hands and stared at a stream of unknown faces. The chatty man next to them met his grandkids. And some Dutch and some Germans picked up their own guests. The throng was departing, the stream returning to a trickle. She twirled at her rings. They weren't coming. They hadn't made the flight.

Then there they were, Nick first, trudging through, shoving at the luggage trolley, still with that same bloody slouch on him, a rolled-up newspaper – a broadsheet, he called it – standing wonky in his jacket pocket. He had a bit of salt and pepper in his hair, Nick, but otherwise he was just him, a great big thing, always second best. And then there was Jo, the mother of her grandson, wrapped round by some thick grey cardigan, the first time Laney'd clapped eyes on her in the flesh, and she looked... But hang on, where was the boy? Where was Fred? Laney felt the life drain out of her.

He hadn't come. They hadn't brought him. Then she saw him, his legs at least, the bottom of them, hanging off the side of Jo. She was holding him. Little Fred was sleeping.

Jo had spotted Laney and Tony now, and she nudged Nick, who smiled and looked over and changed direction.

'Hello, Mum,' Nick said and went to kiss her.

But Laney didn't answer, instead stared straight at Fred. 'Let's see him, let's have him then,' Laney said to Jo.

TONY

'Oh, Spain's nice,' said Tony as they drove beyond Benidorm. 'But it's not Scarborough.'

Laney groaned from the back seat.

'What?' said Tony. 'What have I done?'

'Bloody Yorkshire,' said Laney. 'Bloody Scarborough.'

Laney had her front up. He did himself a bit too. It was like they were playing at being themselves, exaggerating because they had an audience. That's what happened when you rattled around on your own for too long. You didn't have those little collisions with others that smoothed out your wrinkles. You went into storage.

'Some of the smaller ports on the Baltic reminded me of Scarborough actually,' said Nick. 'When we were out there last year.'

'Right!' said Jo. 'I remember you saying.'

'Bloody Scarborough,' said Laney.

'Benidorm,' said Tony, acting the tour guide, 'has the highest concentration of sky-scrapers of anywhere in the world, outside New York.'

'Really?' said Jo. 'Tall town.'

'Tall story,' said Laney.

'It's true.'

Tony looked over to Nick in the passenger seat. He was peering over towards Benidorm, its blocks of huge glinting hotels. 'Pig pens,' Nick dead-panned. 'Vertical kennels.'

'You'd be surprised,' said Tony. 'Not what you think, Benidorm.'

'How come?' asked Jo. 'Nick thinks the place is full of bulldogs and tattoos.'

'Bulldogs with tattoos.'

'There's a bit of that,' smiled Tony. 'But go there in the afternoon, and you see old folk, dressed up with sequins and squeaky-clean shoes, waltzing together in the afternoon.'

'Proper dancing,' said Laney. 'Not on your own like your lot. They dance with each other.'

Tony eyed Laney in the rear-view mirror and tried to catch her eye.

'I'd love to go,' said Jo.

'So would I,' said Tony.

'We *do* go!' protested Laney.

'I mean to dance,' said Tony.

'The dance of death,' said Nick.

'Charming,' said Laney.

'Oh I do like to be beside the seaside,' sang Tony.

'Shush,' said Laney. 'You'll wake Fred.'

'Don't worry. He'll sleep through anything,' said Jo.

'Apart from the night,' said Nick in the passenger seat.

'What do you know, Fatty?' Jo asked. 'When was the last time you got up?'

Tony smiled to himself. She was a bit bossy, this Jo kid, born with her elbows out. Tony had noticed that when he'd been over to stay with them. He didn't mind it too much – Nick sort of needed it – but he wouldn't like it if she turned it on him.

Jo and Laney were sandwiching Fred in his rented kiddie seat. Laney kept glancing at him. The picnic they'd made for the car had gone. All apart from sleeping Fred's bit, which they'd saved in case he woke. They were on the coast road now, not far from the valley.

Jo was looking from one window to the next, eyes bright and darting, drinking it all in: the Med dotted with pale white sails on one side, the low hills husky with light on the other. She still had her big cardie on, her fingers laced across her belly. 'Beside the seaside, beside the sea,' Jo whistled to herself.

Tony looked at the road again, then glanced over to Nick in the passenger seat. He was looking straight ahead. Tony wanted to reach out to him but he didn't know how, so he reached for the currency of football. 'Leeds United are turning it round,' he eventually said.

'I've not been following,' said Nick.

'His hands are so lovely,' said Laney. 'So titchy tiny.'

'Good hands, like his dad,' said Jo.

'I could just make a bloody sandwich out of him,' said Laney.

'They're a state in the boardroom still,' said Tony. 'But they've a bright young manager.'

Nick looked out of the window. Tony turned off the coast road and the whole valley just swung out in front of them, a plane of vineyards centre, a last bright swatch of sunlight bursting across them like orange juice, and the olive and the fig trees on the flanks of the hills shadowed and purple and still.

'Wow,' said Jo. 'Great place for it.'

'For what exactly?' asked Nick.

'Holiday,' said Jo. 'We really appreciate you putting us up.'

'Don't be daft,' said Tony.

'Such pretty hair,' said Laney. 'Lips are like a little bow.'

'I used to call Laney's parents Mum and Dad you know, Jo. You could...'

'Gets dark very quick here,' said Laney, pointing out the window. 'Sometimes just like that.' She clicked her fingers, and it was dark by the time they pulled up at Viva. Nick climbed out and had a stretch. Tony saw him glance across the square to Pepę's, which was heaving, dark heads bobbing this way and that. Tony didn't need to look over to Viva to know what was going on there. It would be rammed, like normal.

The car stilled. Tony got out and walked round the back, popping the boot to get at the luggage. He looked again at Nick, still staring across the square. Tony knew what he was thinking; he had a thirst on, Nick, always. Jo must have been thinking the same. She climbed out of the car herself. 'Help your dad with the luggage,' Jo said to Nick.

Tony smiled a bit to himself, wondered how Nick would take his orders. He'd sometimes been touchy, Nick, a bit thin skinned. Take you the wrong way. But not tonight. 'Course, love,' Nick said. 'In a daze. I'll get that.'

'You're okay, Nick. I'll manage,' said Tony.

'No, it's a bastard that one,' said Nick, leaning in to grab the case. 'Paid excess on it.'

Tony relented, moved back. He was glad to be shot of it.

'What you got in there anyhow, Nick? How long you bloody staying?'

It was supposed to be a joke, but Nick didn't laugh, just peered across to Jo. 'She booked the tickets,' he said.

That wasn't an answer, but, 'Oh right,' Tony said.

He pointed to the little door at the side of Viva that led up to the little room. 'That's you over there,' Tony said to Nick, chucking him the keys.

Nick caught the keys with one hand and lifted the case with the other. 'Thanks. We'll be getting an early night then,' he said. 'I'm bushed.'

'Yep,' Jo yawned. 'Exhausted.'

'Fred's waking up,' said Laney from inside the car.

In the morning. Jo plonked the coffee pot on the table by the pub window and sat down.

'Sugar Puffs?' said Nick, holding up the cereal box.

'I found them in the English shop,' said Tony.

'English shop!' said Fred, who loved Tony.

'Haven't had Sugar Puffs for years.'

'You used to like them,' said Tony.

'When I were five,' said Nick.

Tony smiled. Only yesterday Nick sounded like he'd been twenty years in London, but after just one night at his folks' his accent was broadening up again. It was nice. Nick was putting it on, sort of, but it was a little bit natural too.

They were having breakfast in Viva. They could have fitted – just – round the table at Tony and Laney's villa, but they wouldn't have had room for their elbows. No, it was better here, more space. Laney was next to Fred, and Jo was on his other side, still in her big cardie, as though she was suffering through some winter back home. Fred was scoffing on a big bowl of grapes and strawberries. He had a good appetite on him. The sun was lighting up the big front window. Tony watched the two local lasses from the band walk across the square and step into Pepe's.

'Lovely to finally be here,' Jo said, looking out.

'Lovely to have you,' said Tony.

'Years since you've been, Nick,' said Laney.

'Looks exactly the same,' said Nick. 'Frozen in time.'

'It's not though,' said Tony. 'The happy valley's over. No bastard brass about.'

'Tony! Language!'

'Sorry. I mean no brass about.'

'Brass about,' said Fred.

Phew. They'd got away with Tony's swear. Laney gave him a look.

'Sorry,' Tony said again.

Fred stood up on his chair. 'Bastard!' he said. 'Bastard!'

They hadn't got away with Tony's swear.

'See,' said Laney. 'See, Tony.'

Tony looked at Jo, who was trying not to laugh. Nick was checking his phone.

'Bar-steward, you mean, Fred,' said Jo.

'Bastard,' said Fred.

'No. Bar steward,' said Jo. 'Nick?'

'What?' he looked up, caught on. 'Oh, er. Bustard.'

'Bastard,' said Fred.

'Mustard,' Nick tried.

Fred wasn't being fobbed off with that. 'Bastard,' he said.

'Are you going to get married, Jo?' asked Laney. 'Now you've got Fred?'

Nick slammed his phone down on the table.

'Busted,' said Tony.

'Busted,' said Fred.

The table relaxed.

'The valley's not changed really,' said Laney. 'This place could never change. The hills, the sun, the peace.'

'Did you sleep, Laney?' Jo asked.

'Laney never sleeps,' said Tony. 'What about you?' Tony asked.

'*He* did,' said Jo, thumbing at Nick. 'Me and Fred were up a few times.'

'Were you?' asked Nick. 'I didn't know.'

'I slept *all the way to morning*,' said Fred.

'Well, you were up a bit. You can sleep all the way through tonight,' said Jo pecking him on the shoulder.

'What's the plan?' said Tony.

Nobody answered.

'Beach? Mountains? Or do you just want to mooch round the village?'

'Whatever you want, Tony,' said Jo.

'Jo. Don't be daft,' said Nick.

'What?'

'No need to be shy,' said Nick.

Jo stuck her tongue out at Nick, who turned to Tony. 'Jo's been on about teaching Fred to swim. She's brought arm bands and floats.'

'Good,' said Laney. 'Every kid needs to be a strong swimmer.'

Tony glanced at Laney but she didn't look back. 'Day at ours then,' said Tony. 'Round the pool.'

'But...' said Nick, winking at Jo, who blushed a bit. 'Jo can't go in the pool at the moment.'

'Sorry,' mouthed Jo.

'And she were wondering...'

'I'll teach him!' blurted Laney.

'Told you,' said Nick to Jo.

'You sure?' Jo asked Laney. 'I've got this infection. I can't go in.'

'Mum'll do it,' Nick said, 'She taught us, didn't you Mum?'

'Love to teach Fred.'

'Settled,' said Tony. 'I'm happy with that. Means I can keep Viva open.'

'Viva open!' shouted Fred.

'Didn't you, Mum, you taught us.'

'Viva poo poo.'

'Not at the table, Love,' said Jo.

'Poo poo bottom. Viva poo poo bottom,' said Fred.

'Didn't you. Mum?'

'I'll stay up here,' said Tony. 'Get a few coins in the till.'

'C'mon then Freddy-boy,' said Laney, standing. 'Let's get you in the water.'

Laney pushed her arms out to take him but Fred shied away and looked at Tony. Nick looked at Tony too. 'I'll stay on here for a bit, Dad,' said Nick. 'Help clear up.'

'You don't have to,' said Tony. He didn't want anyone around just now – Keith and Pam had a viewing. 'Go and have a swim,' said Tony, but it was clear that Nick was staying.

Nick tried to help but he just kept getting in Tony's way.

'Where's the bin?' asked Nick. 'Where's the cutlery draw? Where do the table mats live?'

Nick tried to help, bless him, the big ape, but he wasn't much cop. And how long was he staying? With three extra mouths to feed – Nick hadn't once mentioned splitting the shopping – it really was a stretch.

Tony chucked the cloth down. 'Come on,' he said, walking towards the door.

'What?' said Nick, glancing up.

'Don't tell your bloody mother,' Tony said.

Nick grinned. 'I knew there was something. You look different. What's going on?'

Tony just walked outside, waited for Nick, locked Viva up.

Father and son walked across the square and down through the village, past the half-finished houses, past the bodega and over the road onto the path that lead to the urbanisation. Tony could feel Nick watching him.

'It's not that exciting.'

'What is it?'

'In fact it's boring.'

Tony swung left towards a villa, glanced round, clicked quickly through a gate, hurried up a little drive and went round the back. Nick followed and they came out onto a paved back garden, wells sunk here and there for a palm tree, an almond tree, and an orange tree. A swimming pool was sunk in the middle of the patio. The mountains were visible all around.

Nick looked at the villa, saw it was empty. 'What's this?'

'Got to clean a pool.'

Nick looked a bit deflated. 'Why all this skulking?'

'Don't tell your mother,' Tony said, walking towards the pool-house with its door still open. He wanted to see if his bird was still there.

'Is Mum still…?'

'Still what?' interrupted Tony, a bit harsh, hand on the door, half listening inside for his little friend.

'You know, what you said, what you told Jo when you came over for Fred's birthday.'

'I forget what I said. What did I say?'

'You didn't tell me, you told Jo.'

'Oh,' said Tony. 'Your mum's fine.'

'Oh right,' said Nick. 'You told Jo she was going mad.'

'I say all sorts of things,' said Tony. 'Senior moments. Can I…?'

'It's just, you seem…'

'What?'

'You're different…'

'I've got to get on,' said Tony. He slipped inside the pool house and knelt down.

He felt a bit woozy. Tony's heart was thumping in his ears. He heard a little flutter from the corner of the pool house. Tony pulled the breakfast bag out of his pocket and tossed some crumbs and crusts down. He heard another flutter.

'You daft thing,' whispered Tony. 'Door's open.'

Tony stood up. His knees clicked, the small of his back ached. He'd have had a little groan if Nick hadn't been outside to hear him. Tony got the pool brush head and its long handles. He stepped outside, started screwing the bits together. Nick was stood by the edge of the pool. Tony was okay now that he'd seen his little bird. He could relax, make the effort with Nick now.

'Leeds are in a mess,' Tony said.

Nick frowned at Tony. 'You said. I don't really follow the football.'

'Oh yes,' said Tony. He looked up. 'Hot today. No cloud about.'

Nick said nothing. He'd try and dig Nick out, show some interest. 'Making any music, son?'

'No.'

'Still doing the musicians' union?'

'No.'

'Here,' said Tony, opening his mouth. 'Pull my wisdom teeth out as well.'

'What?'

'It'd be less painful than talking to you.'

Christ, why did Tony have to go and say that? It'd just tumbled out. Tony wiped his brow. He was expecting his son to flare up, come out fighting like he used to.

'Sorry, Dad,' said Nick. 'I know I'm no fun.'

'Son,' said Tony. 'It's fine.'

'I'm trying,' said Nick. 'It's just, I don't really want to be here.'

'Why did you come then?'

'Jo made me.'

'Why?'

'Fucked if I know,' said Nick. He turned away from Tony and faced the hills and Tony watched Nick standing still in the sun, staring away into God-knows-what. Just like his bloody mum, Tony thought. Lost in a little bloody world of his own.

It was too hot to sleep.

Tony was tossing and turning. They were only under a thin sheet, him and Laney, and with the fan chopping round above them too, but still it was stifling. He heard Laney shift, hoped she might wake.

Things were weighing on him, and he needed her. Not for talk, he couldn't talk to her about his troubles, he could barely talk to himself, but there was something inside him, gnawing at him, trying to get up to him and make itself known.

He didn't want to talk to Laney. He wanted to feel her. He needed her like an animal, like a beast needs its mate. He looked at her shape under the white sheet, saw her sloped hip trailing down to her half-crossed legs. She moved again, stirred. His hand moved towards her.

She coughed, rolled towards him. 'Jo says they're here for a while.'

'What?' Tony rolled away, sat up in bed.

'Jo says they're going to stay in the flat for a few weeks, have a break, see what happens. Nick's got a few little bits of freelancing to do but he can do them out here. She thought Nick had told us.'

'He didn't.'

'I know.'

'But...'

'I told Jo she could do a few hours at Viva.'

'What!' Tony sat up.

'It'll help them out. Nick only earns peanuts.'

Tony didn't want Jo there. She seemed nice and everything but he knew she'd try and boss him. Quite apart from what he was supposed to pay her with.

'If Jo works with you,' said Laney, 'then I can be with Fred.'

Tony could hear Laney smiling as she spoke. 'It'll be nice, Tony... It's good.'

She turned, faced the wall, settled herself. In a moment she was back to sleep.

Tony got up. He left the bedroom, walked down the short marbled hall to the *naia*, unlocked it, stepped outside. He was barefoot. What was happening? So now they were staying. But Nick had said he didn't even want to be here. That Jo had made him come. Family was a bastard thing. What was going on?

Tony walked round the pool to the back of the garden. He sat down on an old ironwork chair, thinking about what he might have been, what he might have done when he was younger, if he wasn't so mindful of family, if he hadn't had to graft for every coin. He'd never had any fall back, except which he himself could provide. He'd just worked: loyal, meek, often sullen. He'd wanted to give the world to them, to her. To Laney. But she was far off from him now, blind to her husband's heart.

Tony looked up again to the cold stars. Each one seemed against him. He thought of his mum's funeral and he thought of his dad's funeral and he thought of his own.

NICK

Nick stared up into the dark. Jo's voice whispered to him across the pillows.

'I saw you,' she said.

Nick rolled round to face her in the tiny bed, more like a single-and-a-half than a double. 'Saw me what?' he asked.

'Saw you trying with your mum and dad.'

'Oh right,' he said. 'That. Didn't get me very far.'

'It did with me, Nick. Keep the faith.'

'In what, Jo? Why are we here?'

'I told you.'

'You told me, I remember. Nice long hols. Fred gets to be with his granny.' But Nick wasn't having it. 'I know you, Jo.'

'*We're all going on a summer holiday*,' Jo sang.

'Shush,' Nick said, looking to Fred in the cot. 'What are you doing?'

'My holiday song. I'm doing my holiday song.'

'It's not an innocent song,' Nick whispered. 'You're not an innocent girl.'

'No!' Jo squealed. 'Fake charges!'

He'd had enough. 'If you think being here with Mum and Dad is making things better, you're wrong.'

'*Fun and laughter on our summer holiday.*'

'It's making things worse. Mum puts me down. Dad's having some mid-life crisis.'

'No, that's you.'

'What? We're on about Dad.'

'But you must know you're falling apart, Nick, held together by booze and me.'

'Pulled apart by you.'

'As if. Anyway, Tony's too old for a mid-life crisis.'

'Something's up, though. Have you seen him? He looks batshit. Batshitter.'

'He's vulnerable. He's having a kind of three-quarter life crises. Hindus call it the transition to *sannyasin*.'

'Bloody great for them. Have Hindus got a word for how mad he looks? Have they got a word for why my left bollock itches but my right one doesn't?'

'Yes.'

'Has anyone *told* Dad how mad he looks? Mum won't have mentioned it. Mum won't have noticed. Laddo's pissed. Everyone else has gone. Those glowing cheeks he's got. Those gleaming eyes. Eyebrows like an osprey's wing. He's *Hammer House of Horror*.'

'More like a prophet.' Jo laughed. 'He's great.'

'Great, is he? My massive smelted arse is he great. Let's talk gr…'

Fred stirred in his cot.

They glared over tensely, breath held. The lad shifted then moaned. He shifted then settled, rolling back into deep sleep. Relief. Nick sank back into his pillow. He listened to his ear scratching the cotton, and to Jo's breathing and Fred's and his own. The balcony door lay open. A car door opened somewhere in the village. A burble of chatter carried up from a distant street. The air was cool and clean. The moment grew long and melted into other moments. He relaxed and remembered wonderful things.

'You in the hotel bath in Toledo,' Nick said. He touched her neck. 'Naked but for rose petals…'

She put her hand on her stomach and rolled away. 'Don't,' she said.

'Christ,' Nick said.

'Fred,' Jo said.

'Singing is okay though.'

'No.'

'Right, I bloody…'

'Not arguing, Nick. Goodnight,' Jo whispered.

'Right,' said Nick.

'I saw you trying, you lovely man.'

But he was not a lovely man, Nick. The feelings he had made sure of that. And after Jo had fallen asleep he climbed out of bed and stood on the small balcony above Viva and looked out across the square. Everything was quiet and still but painful feelings thrashed inside him, like eels wrapping round each other in his stomach.

Nick looked across to Pepe's, still open although it was late.

He glanced back in to the room. The door that opened out to the stairs was three feet from Jo's face, the same again from Fred's cot. He couldn't go out that way.

Nick stuck his hands on top of the balcony's railing and flipped himself over so he perched on the other side, facing backwards on his toes. Nick crouched, then lowered himself, then dropped the few remaining feet to the pavement outside Viva.

He peered inside the pub, closed now and dark, all except for the one spotlight. That light fell across the bar with its fishing nets and crooked plastic lobsters. And to the side of the bar, further back, the light picked out the shape of the old piano. His mum and dad had had enough time but they hadn't recovered. Some people don't. Some damage is forever.

He looked at the stars, drank at the air. Moonlight covered everything. Nick felt the past tightening around him. The anniversary was coming. The past seemed thirsty and huge. History was waiting for them in the coming days.

He turned away from the light and walked across the square to Pepe's.

JO

J o lay in bed, listening to Fred's breathing, listening to her own.

The air was warm, the village was still. Her mind was free and clear.

Jo got out of bed and stepped out onto the balcony. She watched her Nick walk away across the square, beyond the broken fountain, over towards Pepe's lively bar. The bar door swung open, her husband disappeared inside.

Why had Jo done this? Why had she brought them here?

Two things had happened, back to back, one on a Thursday and one on a Friday.

It had started on the Thursday when she was late getting back from work.

She'd keyed the door to their tiny London flat, stepped inside, added a layer to the coat yeti that grew on the clothes hook then took three paces forward into the lounge. Nick was asleep on the couch, TV still blaring, empty bottle of wine on the coffee table. She turned left and walked towards Fred's tiny room. Pushing the door open, she stepped inside. Bunk beds stood against the back wall. While they only had one kid, they were given the bunk beds by her brother Will, and little Fred loved them, spending one night on the top bunk, one night on the bottom.

Today he was on the bottom.

Jo's knees clicked loudly as she knelt by his bed, but the boy didn't stir.

His small, smooth face lay on the pillow, cheeks as pale as a glue-sniffer's, the sparkly line of snot reaching down to his top lip completing the analogy. Still kneeling, Jo reached into her back pocket, lifted out a tissue, expertly scooped the offending trail.

'Sorry to miss your bedtime, Sweetheart. But I know you've got Papa.'

She kissed his head and then left the room, walking to the kitchen.

In the fridge, Jo found the plate of food that had been left for her. They'd been a bit gourmet, her and Nick, until parenthood had yoked their choices to a kid's tastebuds and things were more primitive now.

Jo lifted the plate out. The mashed potatoes were patted into a face with smiley sausage lips. Two spoons of baked beans made up the eyes. The nose was absent. She smiled, popped the plate into the microwave, moved back into the lounge. She looked at Nick's sleeping face, his head adrift across a sofa cushion, snores beginning to build. He was from home, Nick, next village, an old mate of her big brother Will, but she'd really got to know Nick here in London. He was eight years older but she knew most things about him.

There was a ping, but it wasn't from the microwave. A text from her work phone.

It was a bit late for that. A slither of anxiety moved through her.

She took out the phone, a message from the director: *Check your email. Congratulations.*

Jo's heart pinched. Her head swam. Her finger was a rubbery stick as she jabbed her work email open. And there it was. The formal promotion offer.

She closed her eyes and felt the pressure of choice. Would Nick take on more childcare if she took the job? Did she even want it? *Shit.* This time it was the microwave that pinged – her bangers were ready.

Then it was Friday and she left work on time. They had some friends coming round for dinner and the flat was in a state. Plus, she had to tell Nick about the job, assuming he was in the mood. Jo keyed the lock and entered the flat. She coated the yeti, stepped down the hall and chucked her work bag on the sofa. She heard the creak of Nick's chair as he stood up from his desk in their bedroom. He stepped into the hall.

'Hello,' Nick said. 'Just going to get Fred. Do you want a drink? How was your day? Did you speak to Lucy?'

He was like this now he wasn't at work, pouncing on her with questions as soon as she walked through the front door. 'Tea please,' she said.

'I got the booze for tonight,' he said, 'and I got the tickets for tomorrow. And I got this amazing new magic trick with disappearing coins.'

Nick was having one of his good days.

'There's a hidden slot in the base of the mechanism...'

'My tea?'

He headed towards the kitchen. 'There's this secret slot in the base of the mechanism...'

But she wasn't listening. Jo followed Nick into the kitchen, watched him lift a mug with his clever, slender fingers. She had to tell him.

He flicked on the kettle. 'Such a cool trick for beginners. Reckon Fred would be able to do it with a bit of work. Not that he's big on work, being a kid and everything. Do you reckon Lucy's bloke is just going to chunter on about football again all night?' He was chatty, up. He hadn't been like this for weeks. Nick grabbed the milk from the fridge. He dropped a teabag in the mug.

'We need to talk.'

'Oh. What is it?'

The words queued up in her mouth: *They want me to run the whole department.*

And though the words queued up, they didn't come out. She couldn't say it. She wanted a better moment. Things were too bunched up just then. 'Oh, about your dad. I set myself a reminder for his birthday. What are we doing for his seventieth?'

'No way am I going back out to that expat dump.'

'No, I mean what are we doing for a present?'

'Oh right. Doesn't matter. Some crap socks. A cardigan. What can Dad want at his age?'

Love, thought Jo. *Respect.*

'It's not a dump,' she said.

'You've never been, Jo. Little Englanders huddled round their pools, reading English papers, drinking rough plonk, eating roast beef.'

He looked down on his parents, she could hear it in his voice. 'What are we going to get your dad?'

'Leave it with me,' Nick said, which was his way of telling her to drop it. He poured the boiled water into the cup. 'You can fish your own teabag out.' He glanced at the kitchen clock. 'Time to get Fred.'

She watched him step to the front door in two long strides.

You can't just get your dad socks, thought Jo. *Socks won't do for a seventieth.*

Fred was tucked up asleep in bed. The remains of Nick's lasagne lay wounded in the oven dish. Glasses dotted the dining table. Their NCT friends Lucy and Aussie Glen were over. They all knew each other a bit by now but were still on mainly good behaviour.

'So your folks live in Benidorm, Nick?' said Glen.

'Nearer to Valencia.'

'Great!' said Lucy.

'I've seen Benidorm on TV,' said Glen. 'Jesus Christ it's plebby.'

'They *don't* live in Benidorm,' insisted Nick, the wine rising in his voice.

Jo needed to step in. 'How's the new baby, guys?'

'Oh mate,' said Glen. 'Don't ask.'

'The baby's great!' said Lucy.

'Bullshit, Luce, the new baby's killing us,' said Glen.

'It's not, it's great.'

'Look, Nick, Jo,' said Glen. 'Seriously, having two kids is a whole new game of soccer. With one you can man-mark. But with two you have to adopt a zonal system.'

'A what?' asked Nick.

'A zonal marking system… I know everyone says you're supposed to have two critters so they can fight and go out shoplifting together,' Glen said. 'But seriously, go Chinese mate, stick with one. An anxious introvert is better, and much cheaper, than two sociable screamers any day.'

Nick smiled. 'We've talked about it, haven't we Jo?'

They had. Up to a point.

'And we're sticking with one.' He reached over and took her hand. 'We don't want the pressure. With Jo's job being so demanding, I actually don't think our marriage would take another kid,' said Nick. 'We're at breaking point as it is.'

Breaking point? What?

Jo felt a rise of anger. Because yes, granted, it was true that since Fred's birth there were tensions – practicalities crushed intimacy; conversation arrived in lists; spontaneity was just a difficult word to spell. Things *had* tightened. But then again, they were hardly the Old Woman Who Lived in a Shoe.

She gripped her fork, stared at Nick as he held forth to Aussie Glen on what having a kid had cost them, on how having another would break them for sure.

Get over it Nick, Jo wanted to say. *Blind people raise six kids on dust and beans in shanty towns riven with death squads.* But Jo didn't say that. She did not rise up to take the bait. Instead she went deeper. Because there was what people said, and then there was what people meant by what people said.

Yes, Nick was grumbling, and yes he sounded self-pitying, but underneath there were real reasons why he didn't want another kid. This grumpy git routine was a smokescreen, what he told himself so he didn't have to face his true reluctance; what he told the world to distract it from the broken boy beneath.

Jo and Nick never spoke about it – there was a block there in their marriage – but Nick was protecting himself from the past. He was damaged by what had happened in his own family, and Jo got that – his mum and dad were a tricky pair. They were that post-war generation who considered feelings a weakness, saw pain as self-in-dulgence. They had grown up in a world where most adults had undiagnosed PTSD, where intimacy was as rationed as silk.

They swallowed their anxiety and depression, the Metcalfes, like the statins and wine they now daily downed, and when these emotions did come out – as all emotions eventually must – they splurged out fiercely and sideways, in anger or in tears, or else they festered into migraines and ulcers and sullen angry decades.

What had happened when Nick was young had never been addressed. His parents lacked the skills to help him, and it had curdled inside, become a dark part of who he was. And it lay hidden, dormant, compensated for, until becoming a father dredged it closer to the surface.

Jo got that. It was fuzzy time-travel, parenthood, taking you back to when your own cuts were freshest. And Fred had thrown Nick back into the past, thinned his skin, made the safely hidden once-again raw.

'The one good thing about having a second,' said Glen, 'is that you've got a spare if things screw up.'

'Nope. All my eggs are happily in one basket,' said Nick.

Something pinched inside Jo, some gippy feeling.

Straight away, she knew what it was.

'Excuse me.'

She lurched from the table, pelted to the bathroom, flicking the door locked behind her and jamming her knees down either side of the toilet. She threw up.

Oh Christ.

They'd stopped using anything since they'd had Fred, they counted on Nick whipping it out. But this one time he'd forgotten, got carried away. It was funny – you were dead careful before you had a kid, but then after you sort of felt immune, like it wasn't going to happen. But now it had. She reached over for some toilet roll, wiped her chin.

I'm bloody pregnant, she thought.

She stood up, stepped over to the mirror, tried to look at herself, but she couldn't, it was as though her eyes were drifting off her. *Pregnant.* And right after that zonal marking chat, right after the offer for the new job. What was she going to do?

She put a hand on her stomach.

The door started to open but she was close enough to stick an arm out and jam it shut.

'You all right, Jo?'

'Fine, Nick. Just got caught short.'

'Hurry up then.' Nick pushed at the bathroom door. 'I'm desperate.'

You're desperate?

Long after the guests had gone and the dishes had been done and the empty bottles had clinked down into the recycling, Jo stood in her dark bedroom and looked down at Nick, a street light's haze finding its way through the bedroom curtains to pick out his sleeping face.

Fred was asleep next door.

Jo put her hand on her stomach. The family of three was blooming into four. Nick stirred in his sleep, clacked his teeth, groaned.

A second kid though. After what had happened to the Metcalfe's could Nick ever take to a second kid? Her mind whirred and turned in the dark, throwing up fantasies as though they were options. She would leave Nick and bring the two kids up herself in the wilderness.

Or else she would have the kid and quit her job and run off alone to become a cowgirl.

She looked back at Nick, his face buried in duvet, the crown of his hair orange from the light. She touched her stomach again.

Or else she would just get rid of it.

Jo shoved the pregnancy tester into her pocket and walked out of the toilets and back to her desk. The director saw her and came straight out of the corner cubicle, not her usual buttery self, but direct, striding. She made over to Jo's desk. 'You still haven't accepted the job.'

'I know, I...'

'We need to know, pronto.'

'Yes. Sorry. I have to go out. Sorry. A meeting.'

But there was no meeting. Jo stood, pulled her coat off the back of the chair, picked up a folder as an alibi and shuffled off. She left the office without looking back, took the stairs to avoid the busy lifts, left the building and stepped out onto the pavement.

The street was dour and busy. Jo felt weak and alone. She needed love, needed support.

Jo texted her big brother Will, he was as comfy to her as a cauli cheese – the only member of her birth family that wasn't dead or horrible or drunk, or horrible, or horrible. The only living person that knew.

Will was in so she took a tube then a bus and within an hour she was sitting in Will's home office in the small back garden of his Victorian semi.

'So?' he said.

I'm pregnant, she wanted to say, but the words didn't come out.

'I got the job,' she said instead.

'No surprise, sis.'

'Yes, but will Nick step up and pull more weight with Fred?'

'He does a lot already.'

'Yes, Will, you're right, and I know Nick is your mate but he's resentful sometimes. Half-arsed. Kind of absent.'

'That's pretty critical.'

'There's something in him. Often with Fred, he's *not quite there,* you know.'

'So you wouldn't really want him to do more childcare then, if you took the job?'

'I don't mean that.'

'So you *would* like him to do it, but just *in the way* you want it done. That's being a control freak, Jo. It's called micro-management.'

'What I want is for him to be happy doing it. For him to enter it with glee.'

Will laughed. 'Nick is not really *Mr Glee.* Never has been. Even when we were kids he had one foot in the shadows. Because of what happened, I guess. Unless he was playing. He was happy then.'

'He used to play for me when we first got together.'

'He doesn't anymore?'

'Never.'

'Shame.'

'It is.'

'You're asking a lot, Jo. You want him to be happy and to parent with glee. You want him to get kid puke on him with glee. Receive tantrums with glee. Be isolated from adult interaction with glee.'

'I want him to be reconciled to what happened.'

'Why don't you just tell him then?'

'We've been through this a thousand times. I can carry it and he can't.'

Will gave her the disbelieving look she'd seen many times before, but he did not press matters. 'If he could be reconciled, do you think he'd be a better dad?'

'Yes.'

'And you wouldn't feel guilty about fucking off all hours and leaving him to it?'

'Will!'

'You wouldn't feel guilty about abandoning Fred?'

'I'm not abandoning Fred.'

'I don't think you are. It's you that thinks you are, Jo.'

'I don't.'

'You do.'

'You're right, I do. I think.'

'Is Nick a bad dad?'

'No. No! It's just that he could be better. He could be less fucked up as a person.'

'Which might fuck Fred up less?'

'Yes. Potentially.'

'So why don't you sort him out?'

'How?'

'Why are *we* fucked up, Jo?'

'Because of our mum and dad.'

'Right. To sort Nick out you need to sort his family.'

'Christ. I can't do that,' she said.

*

There was a café down the road from the office where cabbies still hurled back mugs of tea while reading tabloids. It didn't serve lattes. None of her colleagues would be in there. Jo got there early and she headed inside. She got herself a brew and a plate of egg and chips and sat down.

She picked some cutlery out of the pot on the table. Why hadn't she accepted the job?

She speared a chip with her fork, jabbed the chip into her egg, caught a smell of the yolk as it burst. Her stomach turned. There was the baby, doubling and doubling every moment inside her. She stared at the yolk as it oozed from the wound of its broken skin. Her stomach turned again. She pulled out her phone, looked at the screen, scrolled to a new contacts entry.

AC, the new entry read.

Could mean any number of things. But it didn't. It stood for Abortion Clinic. She stared at the number, dialled, hung up, dialled again, hung up again, her stomach churned, the yolk trickled across the plate.

What was she going to do? It wasn't in her plans, and Nick wouldn't accept it. Given his history. Unless she could help him get over it?

But that wasn't easy. She was hardly a model of psychological well-being herself. Besides, nobody stood alone; every tangle in a person trailed back generations. As Will had said, Nick's problem was a problem of his whole family, and Nick's bloody family were in-laws to be the death of you. She could never help that stubborn bloody rabble.

What was she going to do? She was cornered, trapped. Her heart was booming, working away for two, a bomb ticking down to detonation in the maternity ward.

Come on, Jo, what are you going to do?

Why couldn't she think?

She stared at the letters *AC* on her phone.

What are you going to do?

AC.

She closed her eyes, opened them again, looked at the oozing yolk. *Fuck it.*

She called the number, made an appointment.

Jo was stood in the director's corner cubicle.

'So,' the director said. 'I'm afraid that if we don't hear today we're going to offer the job elsewhere. I feel, we all feel, that we've waited long enough.'

'Yes,' said Jo. 'I can understand that. I've had a lot to think about. But now I can answer.'

'Good,' said the director, standing, waiting by the office window.

Jo paused. The words weren't coming.

'Are you okay?'

Jo felt the sickness from inside. She put her hand to her mouth. She pointed at the director's bin beside her desk. 'Can you pass?'

'What?' said the director.

'Bin.'

The director handed over the bin and Jo grabbed it and bent her knees and quickly yacked in it and then wiped her mouth and then stood and looked at the director.

'I see,' said the director calmly and kindly. 'I suffered a lot of sickness myself.'

'It's pretty bad.'

'Is this why you're dodging the job offer?'

Jo nodded. She thought she was in for a roasting. The director looked right at her. 'Do you want a cuddle?'

She did. Jo nodded.

The director stepped forward and opened her arms and gave Jo the most careful hug, like she was wrapping a wren's egg. 'Hang the job,' the director whispered in Jo's ear.

Jo pulled away, and squinted at the director. 'Excuse me?'

'I have three children myself, Jo, and I am desperate to retire so I can be with them more, and with their children. That's life for me. Work is, well, work is just work.'

'But what about us?'

'Us?'

'Women. The gender balance, women getting on in the workplace.'

'The workplace is rotten, Jo. I see you here late every night. Go home, start a business with your baby on your knee. That's what I'd do if I was thirty years younger.'

Right.

'I have to go,' Jo said.

'Of course,' said the director.

Jo turned and darted from the cubicle and across the office and out into the lift and down and out onto the pavement where her arm jumped up to hail a passing cab. She pulled out her phone. Nick was in the park with Fred.

It was grey when Jo climbed out of the cab. Fred and Nick were under the trees by the slide. Fred was sparko in the pushchair, mouth tilted fly-catchingly open. Nick was next to him on the bench. He looked like shit. He'd stayed up late after Jo had gone to bed last night and necked a second bottle of wine. She'd heard every guzzle. Baby monitors don't just work on babies.

'Hi,' said Nick. 'This is a bit weird.'

She said nothing.

'I mean, seeing you on a work day, in the light. It's been a while.'

She looked at sleeping Fred, looked back to Nick. 'I'm taking a sabbatical.'

'What?' Nick asked. 'Why?'

She couldn't very well tell him the truth, could she? She couldn't say, *I'm having a baby that I know you don't want due to your mangled family past, so to keep that baby and to make you want it, I've just this very minute decided to drag us to Spain to sort out your whole screwed-up family.*

No, she couldn't say that.

So instead, Jo said, 'I want to make some time for us.'

'Time for what?'

'For us,' Jo repeated.

'*Us?*' Nick puzzled. 'What? Sexual intercourse type-thing?'

'Well...' Jo paused. 'I want to go and stay with your mum and dad.'

'You're joking.'

'Bit of down time. You can freelance. Let Fred get to know his grandparents.'

'Let's bugger off, sure, if you need to. But expat land? You've not been to the valley.'

'Fred's never met your mum.'

'Let's not start that.'

'He hasn't, though. A three-year-old kid, never met his granny, except by Skype when she's pissed. His granddad comes over for the night with a little suitcase for Fred's birthday once a year...'

'It's weird I know. Why get closer to it? You want a break, Jo. Fine. We can go to Corsica, bag some villa on an olive-clad hillside. A lodge in the Atlas Mountains.'

'We're going to Spain.'

'Andalusia maybe. Toledo again,' Nick smiled.

'To your mum and dad's.'

'It's naff. Do you want Fred to grow a beer belly and read a red top?'

'Snob.'

'What?'

'Your mum and dad live over there and you're looking down your nose.' Jo pinned Nick with a glare. She wasn't letting this go. She absolutely had him. She knew just how to get him on the plane. 'Nick went to university and got himself a laptop and a latte and learned how to spell *structuralism*, and now he's got a posh wife and thinks he's better than his family. Knowing how to make hummus doesn't make you a better person.'

'What?'

'You were born into it but now you think you're better than it. You'd rather the white trash just stayed out of sight. Right little Blair you are.'

'I'm not Blair.'

'New Labour's better than old Labour. Guacamole beats mushy peas.'

'Bollocks.'

'You're ashamed of your mum and dad.'

'Total. Fucking. Bollocks.'

'It isn't.'

'It is.'

And then she just said it. 'Prove it then. Come to bloody Spain.'

BREAKFAST

TONY

Tony felt nervy, like something was going to happen, some boulder that had long jammed up a hole was going to get shoved aside. He crossed the road and passed the bodega and the half-finished flats, trudging up through the village, empty sky following him along narrow streets, balconies drizzling from just-watered plants. The widow who ran the tobacconist was scrubbing her step, an apron strapped around her. She glanced up at Tony and muttered, *'Pirata de Gibraltar'*, then looked way.

It was Jo's first shift at Viva and Tony was dreading it. Jo was smart. She'd find out the pub was bollocksed and he was lying to Laney. She'd sniff him out in about three seconds. And what could Tony do with Jo, anyhow? There was no work to do. And nothing to pay Jo with for not doing it. To sell his bar he had to take customers off Pepe, and his new weapon to do that was some bossy, posh lass who'd served about as many chicken in a baskets as he had psychology degrees. Laney had landed them in a right pickle. It was bloody sabotage.

Tony stopped in the shade outside Pepe's and looked past the white-washed church across to Viva. Jo was stood there, bold as brass. She had her big cardie on and she was sponge-washing the plastic chairs. She had all the chairs out on the pavement and was crouched down, going at them with hot, suddy water.

'Hello,' she said, standing up slowly and smiling.

Tony smiled back. He wanted her to piss off, but at the same time he couldn't help it. He liked the kid. He took a breath and walked over.

'Chairs seemed a bit sticky, Tony.'

'Not that sticky. Done them myself a couple of weeks ago.'

'Not sticky at all then. Just trying to find work.'

'Right,' said Tony. 'Good.'

'There's nobody in,' Jo said, wafting her hand at the entrance to Viva. 'Is there usually nobody in? You don't need two of us on if there's nobody in.'

'It varies,' said Tony, pushing past, 'as to the number of people we have in.'

It whiffed of cleanness inside as well.

'I've done the bar,' Jo said, following Tony in, her rubber gloves lumpy with suds.

'Oh right,' said Tony. 'I'll do the kitchen then.'

'Done it.'

'Gents then.'

'Done them already. There's been nobody in.'

'Oh right,' said Tony. She was doing his head in. She was dead nice and everything, but he really didn't want her there. 'I've got to pop out. You'll be alright on your own?'

'Yeah. Fine,' she said. 'There's nobody in.'

'See you then.'

'See you, Tony.'

Tony turned and walked out the door he'd come in by not one minute before. But then he paused and turned again. He had that feeling again, that some big old stone was about to move. He walked back inside.

'What are you doing, Jo?'

'Thought I'd finish this, then start a stocktake.'

'A stocktake? Right…' He just stood there.

'What is it, Tony?'

Well, if she was asking… But where would he start? 'Nick says he doesn't want to be here. That you made him come.'

'Oh,' said Jo. 'He told you that.'

'What are you doing, Jo? Dragging your family to Spain so you can scrub chairs in some empty bar. How many degrees have you got?'

'Too many.'

'Right. You could be running the world.'

Jo laughed. 'But I am running the world, Tony.'

'What?'

'Depends what you think the world is.'

'It doesn't add up. What are you doing? It doesn't make sense.'

'But that's not the right question, Tony, "Does it make sense?". The question is, do you trust me?'

'What?'

'Do you trust me, Tony?' Jo asked and smiled.

Tony scratched his head. He frowned at Jo then turned around. *Did he bloody trust her?*

He didn't want to be dealing with this. He stepped outside and walked across the square towards Pepe's. A village kid, one of the rough and tumble lasses from the band, was sitting under the shade around the broken fountain, her trumpet case by her feet. She looked at Tony and pointed at Viva and said something to him as he passed.

'No hablo espagnol,' Tony said, not looking back.

Whatever she was saying, he was bound to be getting it in the neck one way or another. He was bound to have cocked something up. Tony stepped into Pepe's. He walked by the TV, past old Chico, sitting in the corner by the rubber plant, playing cards in his slippers, ignoring the expats.

Tony looked out through the window across the square towards Viva. Jo was still outside scrubbing the chairs. Tony moved out of her view to a table facing the bar. Five or six other tables were taken. Consuela with the huge hennaed hair and sleepy Gabriel the mayor were sitting in the far corner. Gabriel was peering into an open pepper mill with his trousers tucked into his socks. He glanced at Tony and then glanced away. Consuela was texting.

Tony looked for a waiter. He needed coffee.

He couldn't pay Jo. But he couldn't stop her working either. Do that and it would get out about the hole they were in. He couldn't do that to Laney. Not with her condition.

Slap!

Tony looked down to see a piece of paper on the table in front of him. The paper had squiggles written on it, numbers it seemed, a long line of them. Tony looked up from the paper to the shape standing in front of him. It was Pepe. He held two small beers.

'Hello, Tony.'

'Hello, Pepe,' said Tony. He pointed at the piece of paper. 'What's this?'

'Your son's bar bill.'

'What?'

'He came here last night. He had no money.'

'Oh Christ.'

'No problem. I covered it, of course. But I wanted you to know.'

Tony grimaced, looked towards the window. 'He doesn't want to be here.'

'Who?'

'Nick, he didn't want to come to Spain.'

'With his parents and wife and child. I am not surprised. Lots of roles, Tony. Looking up to the old, down to the child, across to the wife. Some shitty bits of work to do on his computer. And supposed to be grateful, and supposed to be on holiday. Jesus.'

'Maybe.' Tony frowned. 'But that's life, kiddo. You just have to wear it.'

'Plus there is the past.'

Tony winced. He had spoken to Pepe about it. The only person he ever had, Laney included, apart from an aunt who was long dead now. Pepe sat down opposite Tony and slid one of the beers across the table to him.

'Too early for me,' said Tony, eyeing the beer.

'Me too,' said Pepe, taking a long gulp.

Tony laughed and took a gulp himself. 'Cheers, Pepe.'

Tony picked up the bar bill, looked at the total, stuck it in a pocket, then reached into another pocket and pulled out his wallet.

'Tony,' said Pepe. 'No.'

'My son,' said Tony.

'My bar.'

Tony ignored Pepe. He slapped two fifty euro notes down onto the table.

Pepe left them sitting there between them. Tony left them too.

'What did Nick do? Were he alright? He didn't cause any trouble did he?'

'He was singing.'

'Oh right. What were he singing?'

'Church songs. I do not know them but I am sure that is what they were. Choir boy things.'

'From the past,' said Tony.

Funny lad, Nick. All moody and gruff, but then get some beers in him and he could turn back into that sweet little choir boy.

'How is your painting?'

'Magnificent.'

'How's Lita?' asked Tony.

'The same,' said Pepe. 'Standing between me and myself.'

Tony blew his cheeks out. Could something stand between you and yourself? It was a weird way of thinking.

They were eating outside.

Drunk Nick swung the big pan over and landed it down on to the table.

Tony's wine went splash.

The wine glass rolled across the table but did not break. The hurled wine flew and landed. It missed Tony's trousers but splattered across the patio tiles.

'Bollocks,' said Nick.

'Bollocks!' cried Fred.

'Scallops, I mean.'

'Bollocks,' said Fred.

'Pollock?' tried Nick.

'Bollock,' insisted Fred.

'*Jackson* Pollock?' Jo hedged.

'Jackson's bollock,' Fred replied.

'Bollard,' said Tony.

'Bollard,' agreed Fred, grinning at Tony.

Tony winked at Fred. 'Get you later, monkey face.'

Fred dipped down under the table, emerged out the other end near Laney and ran round to the far side of the villa. He'd eaten before, Fred, an hour ago, taken one look at Nick's paella, called it 'Daddy poo food,' and demanded the pizza which he very quickly got.

Tony watched Fred scamper off. He saw Nick look at the spilled wine. Tony looked at the spilled wine. Laney looked at the sun. Tony supposed he'd better get a cloth.

'Got it,' said Jo. She held a cloth from the summer kitchen and stepped over to mop the wine. *Good lass.* Tony budged out of her way. He looked down to the pan on the table. Nick may have necked the best part of two bottles of wine while he cooked, but the grub looked good. Tony had to give him that.

The turmeric and paprika were as gold and red as the Spanish flag, the meat glistened, and the beans looked plump with flavour. He could cook, Nick – he'd always had a feel for it, ever since he was a lad hanging round the kitchen in some little apron, desperate to do something with Laney. And today he'd made a special meal. Although it'd been Jo's idea to cook, not Nick's. A celebration meal to say thank you to Tony and Laney for having them.

The paella had been cooked in one of them extra big pans.

The recipe had specified the need for it, the big pan, although Tony and Laney did not themselves have one. So Laney had fetched the pan, and paid. Meaning he had. Same with the saffron. Apparently the recipe said you couldn't have a pack of seasoning from the supermarket. Said you had to have fresh saffron.

Fresh saffron. *Bloody hell.* As though he were some emissary from the Spice Islands, some prince or caliph or nabob who could just summon such a thing, call for fresh saffron like it was nothing more than a pack of nuts. But of course Laney had found it. And of course Laney had paid. Meaning Tony was paying for his own thank you meal. At least that's how he felt.

'Looks gradely, Nick,' said Jo, nodding to the pan as she worked away at the wine spill.

'Gradely?' Laney piped up from her sun trance. 'That word takes me back.'

'My nan used to say it,' said Tony.

'How come you can speak like us Jo,' said Laney, 'when you're all hoity toity?'

'Nick went to university too,' Jo said.

'Not a real one,' said Nick.

'My bloody wallet thought it were real,' said Tony.

'It wasn't very good, Dad. Hairy malcontents preaching grudges in portacabins.'

'Now he tells us. Should have gone to Oxford like Jo,' said Laney.

'What was it like, Jo?' Tony asked. 'Bit Jeeves and Wooster?'

'Oxford wasn't built for me. First it was made for monks and then it was made for empire and now it's a status laundry for the scions of the elite.'

'Bravo,' said Nick.

'A bit rhetorical,' Jo said to Nick. 'Bit old Labour. Missing the main point.' She turned to Laney. 'Oxford was made by men for men.'

'Right!' said Laney. 'Burn that bloody bra.'

'I have,' said Jo. She pinched the sides of her cardigan together in front of her stomach. She rinsed the stained cloth under the tap of the summer kitchen, wrung it out, shook it, hung it to dry and sat back down. They all stared at the pan. Unlike a risotto, which you stir, you have to leave a paella alone, the test of a good one being a thick, savoury crust. Jo picked up a wooden spoon, jabbed it into the dish. 'What's your crust like, Nick?' she asked.

'Manly,' said Nick.

'Upper,' said Laney.

'Very good, Laney,' said Jo.

Tony was starving. He wanted the food on his plate and in his stomach. He'd been waiting nearly two hours while Prince Nick had tended his precious cauldron, like he were supervising the arrival of life to the planet. What a dong! It was only dinner.

'Come on,' said Tony.

'You can't rush paella,' said Nick. He turned to Jo. 'You remember we had that one that took three hours in Toledo?'

'In where?' said Laney.

Oh Christ, thought Tony. *Here we go.*

'Oh right,' Laney dived right in. 'When were you there then?'

'Ages ago,' said Nick. 'Years.'

'Thought you'd never been to Spain with Jo?'

'We... I... We did come once, yes.'

'And you didn't come to see us?' asked Laney. 'Not cultural enough are we?'

'There were some buildings,' said Nick, 'that we wanted to see.'

'That's not very nice,' said Laney. 'We've got nice buildings.'

'I don't care,' said Tony. 'I'm starving.'

'I'll be mum,' said Jo, and she served the paella. Deliberate about it she was too, a bit serious. She was only being nice to Nick, Tony knew, making a fuss, making him feel good about his cooking, but bloody hell, some of us did it all the time. *I'd like to see Nick cooking up seven days a week*, thought Tony, *cooking when he's tired, when he doesn't fancy it, when there's only a bloody radish and a crisp-roll in the house.*

Tony had it in for Nick. It was that stuff about the bar tab at Pepe's, and all that farting about with the cooking. And Nick still hadn't said how long they were staying. You just didn't do that. You let people know where they stood. It was getting on his wick. All the old stuff too, bubbling up as the date neared. It wasn't like Tony to have a pop at anyone, it wasn't in his nature. But he quite fancied a go tonight.

'Nice,' said Tony. 'What you cooking for us tomorrow, Nick?'

'Got a kind of deadline. I'm working tomorrow night.'

'Oh right, deadline.'

'Yeah. A database.'

Tony tapped the bottom of the pan with his fork. 'Going to be hard getting that crust out the pan. You washing up, Nick?'

'I'll do it,' said Laney.

Eh? Bloody hell, Laney with her hands in the sink. A miracle. 'You'll what, Laney?' asked Tony.

'I don't mind doing a few dishes,' said Laney, not exactly standing up and getting on with it, but more considering it in theory at this point. 'Let the kids have a nice time. They're on their hols.'

'What about your eczema, Laney?' asked Tony. 'What about your head? You've usually got a bad head.'

'Oh piss off Tony, love. I feel nice.'

'You're pissed.'

'A bit of that. I feel nice.'

'Don't do the dishes Laney. The moon'll fall from the bloody sky.'

'You're being mean.'

'The earth'll plummet…'

'I've had an idea for the pub,' Jo said.

Tony stopped. Laney looked over. Even Nick looked over his wine glass.

'Oh right,' said Laney, a bit of frost in her voice. 'Didn't know we needed any.'

'It's just it were so quiet in Viva today.'

'There are days like that, Jo,' said Laney. 'But it all evens out in the end.'

'It was *very* quiet, Laney. Pepe's was taking all the trade.'

'We do alright, don't we Tony?' said Laney.

He was buggered if he was answering that.

'It were just one day, Jo,' Laney said again, closing down the conversation.

But Nick wasn't having that. 'What's your idea, love?'

'Doesn't matter,' said Jo.

'It does, Jo.'

'Stop it, Nick.'

'No, if Mum and Dad think the pub is perfect already…'

'Shush, Nick,' said Jo. 'It's just a daft idea.'

'Okay. Fine. If Nick wants to hear it,' said Laney, getting bolshie and pretending she wasn't. 'Let's hear your idea, Jo.'

'Really, it's fine. It's just daft.'

'Best ideas often seem daftest,' said Nick.

'Come on,' said Laney. 'Out with it.'

'I thought we could do a new breakfast thing,' said Jo. 'Best bits of the English breakfast, like sausages and bacon. But alongside the best bits of the Spanish. Tortilla and that tomato sauce they do.'

'Oh right,' said Laney, a bit sniffy.

'We could call it *The Full Spanglish*.'

'What!' Nick snorted. 'You're right, it is a daft idea. Worst of both worlds.'

'Told you,' said Jo, flushing.

'We have tried various breakfasts,' said Laney. 'All a little more thought through than yours.'

'Okay,' said Jo quietly.

They were a couple of bastards, thought Tony, picking on the girl like that, shooting her down for trying.

It wasn't right. He wasn't having it. He supped at his glass. He was feeling a bit turvy, a bit loopy, like all his bubbles were pushing to the top. He looked at Jo. What was that she'd said to him at the bar earlier? The question wasn't if it made sense. The question was did he trust her...

'I bloody love it,' Tony said, even though the idea didn't make sense.

'Oh right,' said Laney, looking a bit puzzled, a bit put out.

'Brilliant, Jo. Brilliant,' said Tony.

'Brilliant, Mummy,' cried Fred, running back round from the villa's far side.

Jo laughed, embarrassed. She grabbed at Fred and cuddled him. She didn't look sure if Tony was messing or not. It was the first time he'd seen her anything but in charge.

'We'll do it,' said Tony. 'Tomorrow.'

'Really?' said Jo.

'Really,' said Tony. 'I trust you.'

*

'It wasn't just that stuff about Toledo, Tony. Because I was pals with her until then. I was burning my bra. What was all that about a new breakfast?'

It was night time. Laney was still skittering about, coming in from the en-suite into the bedroom and back again, getting ready for bed. Tony was uncomfy, propped up on his pillows. He was reading, pretending to read at least. The book was called *Yorkshire's Oldest Trees*. It was a niche book, Tony knew. Limited interest. It had a painting of a sycamore tree from Otley Chevin on the cover and when he was young he'd picnicked under that tree at least ten times. He'd lashed it with sticks, peed from its branches.

'This breakfast idea of Jo's.'

He stared at the sycamore on the book cover. He pretended that he hadn't heard Laney. Not that she'd leave it. She'd say it again. It wouldn't take long. When he looked up next she was standing in the en-suite doorway. 'It's daft to do breakfasts.'

'Oh right,' Tony said. He wouldn't be drawn. He knew if he said one word he'd have to say a thousand, the mood he was in.

She skittered off again. But he knew she'd have another swoop. Though she'd better be careful. He looked from his book to the single framed photo by his bed. It was them, Laney and him, holding hands outside the church on their wedding day, the huge yew tree behind them.

Good kids they were back then, him and Laney.

Tony looked away from the photo and back to his book.

'We've tried loads of breakfasts, Tony. I mean she is nice, despite Toledo. We've tried loads of breakfasts.'

He clung on to his book instead of speaking. He'd opened it now and was looking at a painting of a red oak. He looked at it for ages. It stood on a roundabout near Menston. But before the roundabout was even there, Tony had climbed that tree with his best mate Tommo.

Tony glanced up. Laney was standing in the bathroom by the sink, facing the mirror with her back to him. He could feel the truth climbing in his throat, trying to get out of him. The truth about the past and how it had buckled their present, how they spent all their days tiptoeing around what was most clear.

'You know we stopped doing breakfasts because nobody came in,' she called over her shoulder, taking out her earrings and placing them on the shelf above the sink. There was a tube of cotton wool pads hanging beside the mirror, and she pinched one out from the bottom. She reached up to the shelf for her remover.

'Don't do breakfasts, Tony,' Laney said. 'It'll muck with our lie-ins.'

Our lie-ins? thought Tony, gripping the covers of his book. *I've never had a bloody lie-in. You've snaffled every single one.*

It was happening. They were going to turn Viva round, beat Pepe's, and get Tony home. That was the plan. Although Viva was empty and Tony had already counted thirteen people walking into Pepe's. Including Laddo and Shirl.

He was inside, chucking new tablecloths across the tables. Jo was standing outside on the pavement in the morning sun. She'd made a little sandwich board out of kiddies' blackboards that she'd got from the hundred peseta shop, the euro shop as it now was. She'd stuck them all together to make one bigger blackboard to stand outside Viva. She was holding her cardie closed across her tummy with one hand and in the other she had a piece of chalk. She was writing *The Full Spanglish* in big curly letters.

Tony walked out and stood next to her.

'Looks good,' he said.

It didn't; the writing was wonky and the blackboard looked amateurish, but he didn't see anybody else out there making the effort. Tony liked the kid. She was a laugh and you never had to say anything twice. She had gumption, the kid. She had guts.

Tony clapped his hands together. 'Right. Kickoff.'

'We'll get this pub going,' said Jo.

'Oh, right,' said Tony, enjoying her spark.

'And we'll get you working as well,' Jo said, so quietly that Tony almost didn't hear.

What does that mean? he thought, as he watched Jo lift her arm and wave across the square, smiling to one of the local trumpeters squatting in the shade by the fountain. Tony saw the village lass stare back at Jo, smiling.

'Come on,' said Jo, heading inside. 'Busy, busy.'

Tony followed her, then walked into the kitchen. He had all the eggs and toms and mushies and that all prepped. He popped his chef's apron on, picked up a knife.

What was that? A noise. He bobbed his head round the arch that led from the kitchen round behind the bar, and scanned across the tables. Jo was shoving a chair into place. That'd been the noise. He went back to the kitchen, picked up the whisk, worried at his eggs. What if nobody came?

Another noise. He leant round the arch, looked towards the door.

'*Buenos días, bienvenida,*' said Jo.

It was two blokes. Tony stepped forward. Young blokes. Spaniards by the looks of it. Oh yeah, he knew them, one worked at that bar in the big village, the other fixed cars for the garage on the coast road. They'd not been in before. Viva was pulling in new folk already.

He was ready to cook a couple of these new breakfasts now, Tony, these Spanglishes, get a toe hold in the war against Pepe's.

He watched Jo walk up to the blokes. They looked her up and down in a way that riled Tony, but she knew what she was doing. She put her hand out to guide them to a table and they walked over and sat down. Tony went back into the kitchen, ready to start cooking. He waited a bit then saw Jo walk behind the bar and pour a couple of beers. 'Not eating,' she said into the kitchen.

Bollocks. They'd probably just come in to check out the new English barmaid, see what their chances were. The door went again, and Tony bobbed his head out, all hopeful.

'Morning,' Laney called.

'Morning,' Jo called back.

'Busy?' Laney asked, though she could see that they weren't.

Tony came out the kitchen and walked over to Laney, perched

on a bar stool from where she could survey the breakfast service, count the number of Spanglishes sent out, a big *told you so* written all over her face.

'Where's little Fred?' Tony asked.

'With Nick for a bit.'

'So you can have a gloat.'

'It's my place as much as yours, Tony.'

Tony peered closely at Laney. 'You been drinking?'

'Don't be daft.'

But she had. On the booze before breakfast. Like the old days, before they'd left England, when it was really raw and it would pour out from her in a vicious plume of drink. She hadn't drunk in the morning for a long while, and he was buggered if he was going back there. He could swallow a lot could Tony, but not this.

'What you bloody doing, Laney?'

'Nothing.'

'Don't you lie…' started Tony, but Laney was saved by the bell. The door went. It was Laddo and Shirl.

'Ey up,' said Laddo, thickening his accent.

Shirl did a happy little wave.

'Here for the new breakfast?' Jo asked Laddo and Shirl.

Tony stared at Laney, daring her to be cruel. He was furious still.

'Already eaten,' said Shirl.

Laddo and Shirl plonked themselves down at the bar, next to Laney. Laddo clonked a hand into a sugar bowl by mistake then shoved his big glasses up his nose with a finger.

'Do us a coffee, love,' Shirl said to Jo. 'I'm bloody gasping.'

'One for Laney too,' said Tony. 'Big one.'

Laney stuck her tongue out at Tony.

'Three, please,' said Laddo.

'Bloody feet are killing me,' said Shirl, kicking off her shoes. Shirl took her big handbag off her shoulder, plonked it on the bar and rummaged around inside. She pulled out a postcard. 'Got this from Pam and Keith back in England.'

'Oh right,' said Tony.

'They're settling in really well.'

'Bet they are,' spouted Laney. 'All them traffic jams. Broken trains. All that shitty weather. A hundred quid for a haircut. Rioting. Pollution. Black snot. That fracking. The whole country's like a bloody grave. I'm glad it's pissing off out of Europe and leaving us in peace in Spain.'

'Er?' said Shirl. 'Pam and Keith asked us to say hello.'

'Hello!' said Laddo. 'But from them.'

'Pam says she hasn't heard a word from either of you since they moved home,' said Shirl. 'She's worried that she's done something.'

Tony looked over at Laney. She looked so sad suddenly, so lost, that the anger cooled inside him. Why was it that him and Laney hadn't been in touch with Pam and Keith since they'd moved home? Pam had been Laney's best friend, but it was like Pam had dropped off the side of the earth, not hopped on a plane back to England.

But they never mentioned it between them, Tony and Laney. It was easier not to talk about things. It was easier never to mention home.

'Coffee,' called Jo, plonking cups down on the bar. 'Wake you all up.'

LANEY

They were walking away from the village into the woods.

Laney hadn't wanted to bring Jo. The lanes, the paths through the woods, they were hers alone. The wild flowers she found – she'd never take more than a few – they were hers alone too. She didn't want Jo there. Jo stirred things up in Laney.

Laney had put her off before, but now, just a few minutes after the third time Jo had asked, they were walking up a dirt path under the pine shade.

'I just assumed it was short for Joanna.'

'Jolene.'

'As in the song?'

'Yep. Dolly Parton. My mum was a big country and western fan. Used to wear her cowboy boots on the school run. When she could get up for it.'

'How come?'

'She liked the country whiskey as much as she liked the country music. Mummy was a drunk.'

Laney didn't think, just blurted it out. 'No wonder you're like you are.'

'Which is?'

Oh bugger, Laney had cocked up. She recovered. 'Grownup. Dependable, you know.'

'Responsible for others.'

'Exactly.'

'I learned the hard way, Laney. We both did.'

'You and your brother...?'

'Will. Real name Willie. After Willie Nelson.'

'Your name's brilliant.'

'You think so?'

'So bloody chic. Imagine being called Jolene.'

'It wasn't so chic when my dad was cracking my mum about.'

'I bet,' said Laney. 'Sorry.'

Laney stripped her fleece off, kept walking up the lane, deeper into the trees. The hill air was clear and clean and the pine sap was musky and rich. They were getting closer to Laney's place. 'What happened with your mum then?'

'My auntie called time on things when I was eight.'

Laney stopped in her tracks. Jo stopped too and the two women faced each other. 'You left home at eight?'

'Yes.' Jo looked straight at Laney.

'And how old are you now?'

'Thirty-three.'

'Never.'

'I am.'

'Bloody hell. What happened with your auntie? If you don't mind me asking.'

'Lots of things.'

'Sorry, you don't want to say.'

'I don't really, you're right,' Jo said. 'But I will say for you.'

'No, please, if you...'

'We got lucky. We could have fallen into the hands of some witch. But Auntie Joan – Mum's sister – and her husband Uncle Brian were great.'

'Great.'

'Brian said *you're welcome* and *my pleasure* and wore a tie under his cardigan, and they were predictable, did the same thing every day, every week, every year, without surprises, without veering off to drink or hurt someone. He was a solicitor and they couldn't have children and they lived in the quietest house in the quietest street.'

Laney was drinking up Jo's story, peering at her face.

'They had books. Metres of them. She was the reader. Though Brian wasn't too shabby himself. God, she knew shit, I mean stuff.'

'Christ,' said Laney. 'Don't worry. Shit away.'

'Her dad, Auntie Joan's, he made her leave school.'

'As was the way,' said Laney. 'Though I couldn't wait to get out myself. Off like a bloody shot.'

'Where to?'

'Oh, places.' This wasn't about Laney. She didn't want to talk about herself. This was about Jo. 'What about this Joan?'

'Brilliant mind. Completely wasted. Taught herself Urdu for fun.'

'She pushed you at school?'

'No. She made me *want* to learn.'

'Where is she?' asked Laney.

Suddenly Jo was looking right at Laney. 'Why won't you go back to England?'

What? What was this? An ambush?

Laney turned and walked off, the blood pounding suddenly in her ears, the past closing around her like a hot mist. She heard Jo behind her. Jo drew level. 'Sorry, Laney.'

Laney was breathing hard. 'That was a bit full on, Jo.'

'Yes. It was... Why don't you go back though?'

Laney stopped walking. She was tough, Laney, she thought she had to be to protect herself. But she looked at Jo. There was something about her, this Jolene Dobson. Laney opened her mouth. Jo had told Laney something that she didn't want to. Laney would do the same. She looked away, started walking. 'Do you know what SAD is?'

'As much as anyone.'

'No, I mean S. A. D. Seasonal affective disorder.'

'Yes,' said Jo. 'Light makes you happy. Get depressed by the dark.'

'Exactly.'

'You've got that?'

'Yes.'

'The doctor said you've got it?'

'Yes.'

'A private doctor?'

'Yes.'

'You think your depression is to do with the sun.'

Laney wasn't quite following what was happening. Jo was being tricky in a way she could not work out. Maybe Laney shouldn't have traded secrets. They were nearing her special place. Laney started scanning the lane for a stone of the right size. She found one, bent down, scooped it up in her palm. The stone felt hard and her mood had hardened too.

Questions not answers now. She kept walking.

'So you met Nick in London?'

'We met properly in London – he was friends with Will.'

'Nick was?'

'Yeah. For years.'

'With a name like Willie I thought I'd have known.'

'He called himself Will. But I'd have thought so too, Laney... My brother and Nick met up for a drink and I tagged along.'

'Right.'

'But I'd met Nick before, at school. I was eight, it was just before. And he must have been sixteen. He was in that band of his, Clotted Horse.'

'Clotted what?'

'And my mate Jane's dad drove us over to your village. I mean we couldn't get in, it was for the big kids, but I saw your Nick carrying his keyboard into the hall and I just kind of stood in his way trying to work out what to say to him but he just walked past me, so we did sort of meet once before, in your village, just before... Before my family were broken up. So we met in London really, because Nick doesn't remember the first time we met with the keyboard.'

They were there. They'd reached her place. Laney felt the stone in her palm, looked into the undergrowth by the side of the lane. Jo stopped abruptly. She put her palm up over her mouth. 'Sorry, I.' She bent over and looked like she was gagging. 'Dicky tum.'

Laney fished a tissue from her pocket and handed it to Jo. 'Thanks.'

Laney looked away to the mound of stones in the undergrowth, the cairn she had piled up, hundreds and hundreds of small smooth stones, every one of them a walk on her own in the woods. Every single one of them – she bent down and added the stone – except this, which was a walk with Jolene Dobson.

'Oh, God, look at them,' Jo said from behind Laney now, recovered and seeing the clearing of meadow grass behind the first row of trees.

The clearing was spotted with wild flowers, bright as spilled paint. Jo walked by the cairn into the clearing, knelt down in the grass, looked round at the flowers. She reached out to touch one, but, 'No picking,' Laney said, because you couldn't just barge into Laney's places and take whatever you fancied.

TONY

The cardboard box was big and heavy but Tony humped it inside and left it in the middle of the pub floor. Its contents had cost some of his last remaining euros, or so it felt, and he wasn't entirely sure he knew what he was doing. Tony watched the delivery van driver back out of the square then he called Jo.

She came out of the kitchen with rubber gloves on and a scourer in one hand, the other pinching her cardie closed across her tum.

'You're getting suds on that.'

'What?'

'Your cardie.'

'What's that?' Jo said, nodding to the box.

'Open it.'

'Great,' said Jo. She wasn't coy. She smiled and walked over.

She stretched the rubber gloves off her hands, popped them on the back of a chair and jabbed a thumb straight into the packaging, wrenching at the tape. It was nice to see her excited. He'd have loved to see her when she was little, opening presents on Christmas morning. She had gusto. She reminded him of someone.

Tony spotted Pepe walking across the square towards Viva. He carried his kit, a paint box and easel wrapped all around him, a couple of canvases bound face-out over his shoulder. One cheek had cobalt blue dabbed on it. Fire engine red was in his hair. He was sweaty and dirty and alive, on his way back from the fields.

Tony walked behind the bar, quickly poured a beer, and met Pepe in the doorway. 'You look like a pirate,' said Tony, handing Pepe the glass.

'Thank you,' said Pepe. He gulped the beer straight down. 'Very nice,' he said, looking beyond Tony to Jo, unwrapping the package on the floor.

Tony turned and saw Jo drag it fully out of the box. It was a new menu board for outside Viva, a big one, one of those with two blackboards strung together at the bottom and touching back-to-back at the top.

'Ta-dah!' said Jo, stepping back. 'Brilliant.'

'Very nice,' said Pepe.

'Begging to have our new menu written on it,' said Jo. 'Brazenly asking.'

'You will put me out of business.' Pepe smiled and handed back the beer glass.

'That's the plan,' Jo said, marching off towards the kitchen. 'I'll get the chalk.'

Pepe reached into his pocket, 'Here,' he said. Pepe held a piece of paper with a column of numbers squiggled down one side. It was a bar bill. Another one.

Tony took the bill from Pepe. 'Right,' Tony said.

'He was nice. He brought money.'

'Good.'

'Then Chico took it off him at cards.'

'What?'

'It's fine, fine. I like him.'

'Why was Chico playing with him?'

'Chico likes him too. He was singing again. Dancing.'

'What?'

'He danced with Chico.'

'Nick danced? Chico danced?'

'Chico *sang*, Tony. Nick and Chico sang at the bar.'

'Our Nick?'

'Drunker than ten New Years, Tony. A pleasure for Pepe's to have such entertainment. A floor show, I think you call it.'

'Give over,' said Tony. 'Never.'

'I was there.'

'Christ,' said Tony. He reached into his pocket.

'Keep your money, Tony, you will need it in the war between Viva and Pepe's.' Pepe looked at the new blackboard. 'The arms race begins.'

'Does it chuff,' said Tony. 'You're my mate.'

'And you are mine,' said Pepe, leaning over and kissing Tony on the head.

Pepe winked at Tony and turned, and Tony watched Pepe walk across the square, his paint box bucking against his hip, a slash of titanium white bobbing visible now and again across the back of his trousers.

'Good luck tonight,' Pepe shouted over his shoulder as he walked by the shaded fountain. 'Everything you want for yourself, Tony my friend, I want that for you too.'

'Thanks, pal,' Tony whispered.

'Only got green chalk left,' Jo shouted from the kitchen.

It was early evening. He was standing alone in the window of Viva, the new menu chalked in green on the new blackboard on the pavement outside.

He had a chef's apron on and a white T-shirt and a chef's hat. His arms were bare. His face was shaved, his ears were cleaned. He'd slicked his hair back and trimmed what Jo had called his 'Prophet's eyebrows'. He looked up to the sky, blue as the sea, with one white star braving the heat already, one white kite flying high above the church.

It was a big night. He had the new menu in his hand.

He flexed it, looked down.

It was nothing to look at, just a handful of dishes written on simple white card. Jo had put the menu together. He'd just left it to her. It put an end to him catering out of the freezer and the deep fat fryer. It was simple stuff that Jo had found in shops and bodegas in the valley. Nothing special, but done right. He reckoned Jo could do it, turn Viva round. He believed in the kid.

Right now she was polishing glasses behind the bar.

Nick was at the back of Viva, tapping away at his laptop.

Apart from them, the pub was empty. Laney was at the villa babysitting Fred.

Tony looked across to Pepe's, saw dark heads bobbing inside, a warm murmur coming off it already. Tony heard footfall outside. The widow who ran the tobacconist clomped slowly into the square. She saw Viva's new menu board and approached, peering at it with interest. The widow took a pair of glasses from her apron and put them on and peered at the menu again.

'*Inglés!*' she tusked sharply, pointing at the board and then at Tony in the window. '*Comida de piratas!*'

She was cross, but Tony didn't invent the bloody English language did he, and he'd hardly gone knocking door to door canvassing for people to vote to leave the bleeding EU.

He'd rather not be there either, eggy tobacconist woman, instead he'd rather be sat beneath one of Yorkshire's oldest trees, say, eating onion chutney and a decent pork pie and listening to *Test Match Special* on his tranny. They were only trying to cook some bloody dinner, they weren't twanging Iniesta's Achilles or knee-capping Don Quixote's horse. They weren't stealing Spain away from under her nose.

He wanted to blow a raspberry, stick his tongue out.

'*Inglés!*' the widow cried. 'Brexit animal!'

Jo walked past Tony and stepped out onto the square, smiling at the grumpy widow. But Tony turned away. He walked deeper into the pub. He had a cob on now. The pressure of the day had set his blood going. Nick was sat at the back of Viva, opposite the piano. He had his head down, Nick. He was quiet, working away at his computer, *freelancing*, whatever they called it.

Which was bollocks as well.

Was anything Nick earned going to find its way towards the food bill, or the petrol, or cover the coffee or the booze? What were these *databases* of Nick's anyway? Tony couldn't see them. They weren't real like cooking a meal was real, or building a wall, or nabbing a robber. Nick's generation seemed to think you should get paid for slightly changing some words while drinking a coffee. But how was that a job? How was that *doing*? You couldn't point to Nick's work like you could point to a big crap you'd just done and say, 'There she blows! That was me!'

Far as Tony knew, Nick might be looking at nothing on his screen.

He might be staring at a basin of tripe, or a dog in a dress. Nobody would twig.

Tony looked at Nick, all beardy and big and crouched over his laptop in the corner like some teenage thing that never seemed to age, except by getting further and further away, and by being able to drink more wine, and by being less grateful and looking down his nose more. Tony looked away. Out of the window, out on the pavement, Jo was talking to the widow and the widow wasn't cross anymore. Instead she was listening to Jo and Jo was pointing at the menu board and then the two girl trumpeters with the scruffy bleached mullets walked by in the square and greeted Jo who waved back and the church clock chimed and Tony heard Nick's chair grate behind him in the pub.

Tony had the drink waiting on the bar before Nick had even arrived.

'Thanks,' said Nick, picking up the glass. 'Read my mind.'
Weren't hard, lad.

Nick had a big glug and put his glass down. 'Dad, I just transferred some…'

But Tony wasn't listening. 'May as well take the whole thing.' He looked at Nick dead straight and then clunked the bottle down on to the bar. 'Take it all Nick, save you standing here. Save you coming back.'

'No, it's okay.'

'No, go on. Take the bottle. Might help you with your work. All them basins of tripe you've got to look at.'

'What?'

'All them dogs in dresses you've got to see.'

'Dad?'

'What do all those tappety taps on your keyboard mean?'

'Dad... It's my work.'

'What is?'

'Building databases.'

'That right, is it Nick? You sit in the corner drinking coffee and wine and you build databases?'

'Dad...'

Jo had come back in now and she was standing by the door, listening. She didn't seem flustered by the conversation. She looked, Tony thought, almost like she was expecting it. Jo laced her fingers across her stomach and watched. And something about Jo spurred Tony on, even though Nick was her bloke, the father of her kid.

'Are you hungry again, Nick? Do you want to try something from our new menu? The menu that nobody's come in for yet. Have it on the house, because the house can afford it, thank you very much for asking.'

Nick was white as a sheet. All the colour had gone out of him.

'I was waiting for an invoice. I would have told you, but actually, fuck it. Do you think I like this?'

'Like what?'

'Sitting here scratching about in some data pen for peanuts while I'm supposed to be on my,' Nick looked over Tony's shoulder, 'hols.'

Tony heard Jo shift behind him.

'Do you think I like having this shit workload follow me everywhere, turn every sunset database grey?'

'Nick, I...'

'Don't you think I'd prefer a world like yours was, Dad, a bit more defined.'

'Defined?'

'The full-time job. With a final salary pension scheme. And sick pay. And, hey, let's throw in some cheap, post-war housing, and low household debt, and a functioning NHS and some roast dinner and the village bobby and Eric and Ernie. Don't you think I'd have fancied the full post-war retire-when-you're-fifty-five, all-inclusive analogue package deal myself, Dad? Instead of this rolling, half-assed anxiety-debt-surveillance shit that my lot got given? This whole trapped in the mossy, shit UK now that your generation voted to piss in the well it had drawn so liberally from. Don't you think I'd prefer a place in the sun and an early retirement?'

Tony got everything Nick said, sort of. He knew where his son was coming from. Only two problems. Nick was wrong and he was also a self-pitying bastard, excuse Tony's French. Tony was in a fury. He'd slipped his bounds. 'But I'm not retired, am I, son?'

'You could be.'

'Know that, do you? Facts at your bloody fingertips, are they? All knowing of the bloody situation…'

'Dad.'

'Summon it up through Google, can you?'

'Er.'

'Discover the valley's best coffee, as rated by bloody Trip Advisor, can you, eh?'

'Dad, what are you…?'

Tony waved his arms. 'You're not the only one capable of cyber war, Nick.'

'What?'

'I can bloody internet, mate.'

'You can what? You're calling me *mate*?'

'Watch it.'

'You're pointing at me and telling me to watch it.'

'I've glimpsed the dark web too, son.'

In walked Shirl and Laddo and Shirl clocked there was a row. 'Careful,' she said to Laddo. 'He's glimpsed the dark web.'

But Tony was over the edge and he just turned and went straight at them. 'You want some food, Laddo?' Tony said. 'We've got a new menu on.'

'No, we've...'

'You've already bloody eaten.'

'We have,' Laddo said.

'Always the same. Always bloody eat before you come out, unless the grub is free. You've got more gold than Gaddafi and you're both tight as a nun's chuff.'

'Tony!' said Shirl. 'You rude bastard.'

'You got a hip flask in that handbag, Shirl? So you don't need to buy a drink?'

Laddo stepped forward. His glasses were all wonky. He was placid mostly, Laddo, but he wasn't renowned for taking too much shit. 'Stop, Tony,' Laddo said. 'Stop.' Laddo held one hand out, palm open, like he was commanding the tide. 'You need to stop, Tony.'

Tony could feel his anger falling back.

'You've been weird about Pam and Keith since they left,' said Laddo.

'Have I?'

'You have,' said Shirl. 'Your Laney has.'

'Right,' said Tony.

'And now,' said Laddo, 'you're on at us.'

'Here, here,' said Shirl.

'You're giving out to us, Tony, but answer me one question.'

'What?'

'Are you sure your problems aren't a little closer to home?'

'What?' said Tony.

'Problems at home,' Shirl said quietly. She waggled her pinkie.

'Exactly,' said Laddo. '*Cherché la femme*, as Keith would say.'

'And the French,' said Shirl. 'Alongside Keith.'

Laddo popped his arm out for Shirl to take, which she did and then they turned and walked over towards the door they'd just come in by.

'Goodnight, Jo,' Laddo said.

'Goodnight,' said Jo.

'Place looks nice,' Shirl said.

'Thanks,' Jo said, staring at Tony, her eyebrows raised. 'We hope you enjoyed your visit.'

Shirl gave Jo a peck on the cheek then stepped outside. Tony slumped. He had bollocksed it all up. He grimaced at Jo, like a sort of apology. He wasn't angry at Laddo and Shirl.

'You okay, Dad?' Nick said, walking towards Tony. 'Why don't you sit down?'

Tony stared at his son. Was he angry at Nick? He was, yes. And he was angry at Laney, and himself. And he was angry at the past, how it still had his family by the chuff.

Tony looked out into the square. His mates were walking into Pepe's.

Later on he locked the pub door and stumbled across the village square and down the hill towards the urbanisation. Tony was too ashamed to go home.

They'd not had one customer for the new menu. Not bloody one. She'd enjoy that, Laney.

Maybe Tony was wrong to trust the kid Jo. Maybe she was making a fool of him. He'd never manage to make any money. He'd never sell the pub; he'd never go home.

Tony felt exhausted. He was pissed. He wanted a drink. He wanted a pee and a cry. He wanted a drink. He felt exhausted. He stumbled down the track to the next-but-one villa, the empty one where Pam and Keith used to live. Tony banged straight through the gate and straight round the back. He walked up to the pool house. The door was ajar, not locked.

He put his ear to the little crack and listened.

He wanted to find his friend, the little bird. He had some crumbs in his pocket from Viva.

He listened then listened again. Nothing.

He made a sucking sound with his teeth, bobbed inside, dropped a few crumbs.

Tony turned the light on, clattering the pool brush.

Bollocks.

He couldn't see or hear the little bird anywhere. Tony shifted a tub aside, budged some old tiles and a paint pot. He looked behind the old brush head.

Nothing. The bird had gone. Left through the open door.

JO

J o lay in bed and watched her husband.

Nick was in his flip-flops, out on the balcony above Viva, staring across the square to Pepe's.

'Nick,' she called to him. He peered into the room. The cot was empty; Fred was staying up at the villa. Jo was laying under a sheet across the single-and-a-half bed.

'Nick,' she called again.

'Hi.'

'Waiting for tomorrow,' she said.

'Is that why we're here?'

'What do you think?'

Nick stepped inside. Moonlight lay across his face and body, muzzed orange by the street light that met it. Nick walked around to her side of the bed. She looked up at him. He touched her face. 'Will you come out, Jo?'

'It's hot,' she said.

'I'll sing for you. We'll dance.'

'Stay in.'

'I'm going to pay my bill.'

'I liked what you said to your dad... Village bobby. Eric and Ernie. Sounded like a Clotted Horse song. Funny how your brain works.'

'*My* brain? I told you he was mad. *I can bloody internet, mate.*'

'*Sannyasin,*' she said. 'He's on the march.'

'You're not helping him.'

'I am,' she said. 'And you.'

'Right.'

'I have two hearts for you, Nick.'

Nick rubbed her temple softly, where the hair met the skin. She knew he didn't understand her. How could he when one of the pieces was kept from him?

'Don't kill Chico,' Jo said. 'Come home safe.'

He bent down and kissed her then she watched him walk away.

Jo lay awake, long after Nick had gone.

They were madder than she'd thought, these Metcalfes. They were more stubborn than she'd guessed. Ideally, to sort them she'd just stand back, stir occasionally, watch the pot boil. But it wasn't going to happen like that. She had to step in now, turn up the heat herself. She might get caught doing it. They were on to her for sure. But Jo had to take the risk.

It was tomorrow.

It was time to shove the Metcalfes over the edge.

Jo closed her eyes, tried to sleep.

REALLY?

TONY

B*ang! Bang! Bang!*
    Tony was only just out of the shower. He was on his way to breakfast when he heard it.

Bang!

Bang!

Tony changed direction. 'Hold your bloody horses,' he called.

Someone was hammering at the kitchen door. It was probably Jo, come to pick Fred up after his sleepover. But she wasn't half early, and she wasn't half going at it. She'd bang the bugger door down at this rate.

Tony took the bolt off. He opened up.

'Viva's closed,' Jo said, as soon as she saw him.

'You what?' said Tony, squinting in the sun that followed her into the shuttered kitchen.

'Viva's closed for the day. We're all going out.'

He closed the door behind her. What was she on about, Viva's closed? No it wasn't. He'd be there in half an hour, he just needed to sort his headache out. He looked at Jo. She was dead bolshie. She was looking right at him. She clearly had some plan in her head. He'd known she was up to something for a while, but it looked like whatever that something was, Jo was pushing it along now, shoving it right up through the gears.

Ey up, Tony thought. *Buckle up.*

He backed off. He'd buy a bit of time. He padded over to the medicine drawer in his slippers, took out some paracetamol and headed to the sink, flicking on the kettle as he passed. What did Jo mean about closing Viva? He was feeling peaky from the drink, Tony, and peaky from the rest. Discombobulated, you might say. Shitting bricks, as his granny had it.

What was Jo doing? He didn't understand but he felt change all around him, like real life was tattering apart as easily as some old newspaper. And there stood Jo, somehow his attacker, but somehow his saviour and his mate, demanding another U-turn from him, calling for him to close his bar.

He assessed her slyly from the corner of an eye. She had a set look about her. Tony didn't know if the look was mad or sane. But whatever the look was he wasn't going to pick a fight with it. May as well grapple a tornado. He took his paracetamol then got three mugs out, pulled the caddy out of the cupboard.

'Not for me,' said Jo. 'Where's Fred?'

'Watching TV.'

'Is Laney asleep?'

He nodded, she was. Despite Tony having been the one who'd worked the night before and then been up until God-knows-when, it was still Laney that took the lie-in and Tony that got up early to be with the kid.

'You go wake her then, Tony. We need her.'

'Who made you head girl?'

She laughed.

'Never occurs to you that you're not in charge, does it Jo?'

'Grown-ups aren't grown up Tony, not many. They pretend to blame others, but really they blame themselves for things. People need shoves to live right. They can be stubborn as donkeys when they get set.'

Tony brayed and Jo laughed. 'You hungover?' she asked.

He nodded.

'Like father, like son,' she said.

'I bloody hope not, Jo. Poor sod Nick, won't want to take after me.'

'Why not?'

'Oh, my day's done, Jo. Remember Nick's speech. *The whole analogue package deal.* I've been gentrified out the bloody picture. It's been digitally retouched. Shove me in the corner, ashamed of me.'

'Not true. Nick should.'

'He should what?'

'Want to take after you.'

'What?'

'You're good. You're brave.'

'I'm not brave, Jo.'

'You bloody will be,' she said.

'Give over,' Tony said, but he smiled. 'Not much cop last night, were it?'

'Shite, Tony. We sold nothing.'

'Right. Nothing.'

'That was yesterday.' She chewed at her lip. 'Today we're off on a jolly.'

'Oh right. Where to?'

'Benidorm.'

'Benidorm? Nick'll flip his lid.'

'We need some lids to flip,' said Jo.

She walked off into the lounge. Tony heard the TV being switched off then Fred start complaining. Wouldn't get him very far with Jo, not today. She came back out holding Fred. 'Off to get Nick,' she said. 'Can you pick us up from the bar in an hour?'

'Yes,' said Tony. He was powerless to do otherwise.

Tony watched Jo and Fred walk towards the door. Tony looked at Fred's little bandy legs. Those bandy legs gave Tony a thought. 'Hang on,' he said. 'Give me five minutes and I'll drive you up.'

Jo turned, smiled. 'Thanks.'

Fred smiled too. 'Granddad,' he said.

Tony still felt a turd about fighting with Laddo, so Fred's smile was precious to him. Like he couldn't be all bad to get a smile like that. Tony was glad to help out, give the lift, despite being the bad end of a skinfull and going without breakfast.

'Give us a bit,' said Tony.

He walked over to the kettle to make Laney her morning brew. She was awake when he took it in. 'Get ready, love,' he said, popping the mug on her table.

'Why?'

'Jo says we're going to Benidorm.' Tony shrugged. 'Pick you up here in an hour.'

'Okay,' said Laney, right as rain. She sat up, reached for her brew. 'Great.'

She was good like that, Laney. She liked surprises.

Which was just as well, given how the day turned out.

The bedroom was dark and small and humid. Tony stood queasy by the door. Jo whisked the curtains wide and sunlight painted the room, brushing across the boulder of bedclothes under which Nick lay.

'Poo poo Daddy,' said Fred who was holding Jo's hand.

'Come on Nick,' said Jo. 'Get up. We're off out.'

'Stinky Daddy,' said Fred, holding his nose.

Fred was right, the room was quite farty.

'Fresh air,' said Jo, yanking open the balcony doors.

'Coffee,' the Nick lump croaked.

'Get up,' said Jo, then she and Fred walked by the bed and out the door. Tony stayed put. He looked at Nick, still covered, but twitching and stretching a bit now.

'Dad,' Nick said, springing up suddenly from inside the bedclothes. 'What's happening?'

'We're going for a jolly.'

'What?'

Tony wasn't going to tell him where to.

'You know what day it is, Dad?'

'I do. Don't you start talking about dates in front of your mother.'

'You think she's forgotten?'

Tony said nothing, just padded out of the small bedroom and padded down the stairs, and out on the pavement he padded to the front door, and unlocked Viva to make Nick a coffee.

After helping his hungover son, Tony went back to his car and drove to the villa to pick up Laney. He rowed with Laney because she wanted to have a picnic but they didn't have time to make it, then he made the picnic himself while Laney put her face on. Then Tony loaded the picnic and the beach kit into the boot, then drove back to the village and loaded up Fred and Nick and Jo's kit too.

Tony stood over the packed boot. The sun was fierce. His head was swimming. He felt like there was sherbet behind his eyes.

'Come on, come on. Get in.' He hurried them all along.

When everyone was in the car he slammed the boot closed and climbed into the driver's seat and started the engine. 'Right,' he said. 'Day out.'

Five minutes down the road he saw he was still in his slippers.

Laney was in the passenger seat. Tony's head was boiling, but it wasn't far now.

Fred started again. 'Poo poo, Daddy poo.'

Jo shushed at him, but he didn't stop.

'Poo poo, Daddy poo. Poo poo, Daddy poo. Daddy is a poo poo.'

Tony had a squint in the rear-view. Nick looked grey, his eyes were red, his fingers were pressing at his temples. Nick looked forward through the windscreen to the high-rise buildings coming into view, the soaring hotels and then apartment blocks huddled by the sea.

'Look at it,' said Nick. 'Bloody Benidorm,' and everyone blurted 'ssshhh' at him for swearing.

'Well,' Nick appealed. 'Look at it. I more or less had to swear.'

'Why?' asked Tony.

'Because it's awful.'

'You ever been, Nick?' Tony asked.

'I've seen a...'

'But have you been?'

'No.'

'Right then, Daddy Poo Poo.'

*

Benidorm has two long beaches in two curling bays, the shape of two raised eyebrows, and Tony parked in a side street on the tip of the furthest bay, right in front of a shop selling ritzy beach goods. As Nick peered unsure out of the car window, Tony climbed out and looked down at his slippers. He kicked them off and chucked them in the car then walked off barefoot into the shop to buy some flip-flops or sandals. As long as they were size ten and under a fiver, he didn't really mind. He chose something and paid, slipping them on at the counter.

The light and the heat were fierce as he stepped outside and looked over towards Laney and the rest, walking ahead along the cracked yellow pavement.

Hang on, he thought, *wait for bloody me*.

He'd just bloody driven, with a banging head, and no breakfast, and they'd just strolled on and left him behind. He zapped the car locked and hurried after.

'Hey!'

They bobbed around a corner and Tony had to put a spurt on. He was out of puff before he'd even started. Panting, he came out onto a main road. To his left was a huge hotel, a high, glassy stack of rooms, beach towels hung in its glinting windows. On Tony's right, across a wide quiet road, was a shop selling glitzy bags and shades and jokey inflatables.

Next was an English expat café with a St George flag flying and the names of the owners, *Dave and Val*, on its sign. The café had a chalkboard advertising English soap operas, Sky Sports, Roast Dinners. He caught up with the rest outside the Loch Ness Disco Pub.

'What the...?' Nick said. His face looked like the whole city was some piece of chewing gum that might stick to him. They walked on. Tony panted. Palm fronds shaded the entrance to The Yorkshire Pudding pizzeria. Nick boggled. A skinny German man, maybe eighty, cycled by in dungarees. There were more palm trees and hotels then suddenly they were out on the sea front, right in the sun, just one road keeping them from the wide, shady esplanade and the beach.

They paused at the road. It was baking. They were mad to be out in it. The Med was a wet slant of blue between a dry blue dome and a singe of yellow sand. Tony was wilting. A taxi pulled up to the kerb beside him. He watched two Spanish women hop out onto the pavement and scuttle for their restaurant, fleeing from the sunshine as though it was rain.

Tony watched them vanish inside the dark cool doorway.

'Too hot,' he remembered saying, feeling his knees go.

Jo stepped towards him and made a grab for his elbow, but by then it was already black.

When he came to, it was like he was in a cave. It was dark and cool.

But what was the place?

He was sat down but his head was hanging backwards. He opened his eyes and above him he saw a dark roof with dark cloth hanging from it. He tilted his chin forward so that he looked ahead. The wall directly opposite was mirrored, reflecting dark tables around which people sat. It was brighter to the left of Tony than to the right and he turned his head left and looked towards the brightness.

He saw sunlight, and in it the pavement and the road and beyond that the beach and the sky and the sea. It hurt his eyes to look towards the sun, so he looked away. He came round more. His arms were holding onto a plastic chair. He was in a café.

At the far end of the café was a bar and a small stage. The bar was covered in stripes of bamboo all along the front, and tall plastic rubber plants stood to either side. On the small stage was a piano. An old woman in light blue slacks and a white polo shirt sat at the piano, but she was not playing. Standing next to the piano were an old lady in a peach cardie and an old man with slicked-back hair. Both held trumpets at their sides as they chatted with the old woman sat at the piano. In front of the small stage was a brightly lit wooden dance floor.

A glass of water was at Tony's lips.

'Drink that.' Jo was holding the glass. 'You fainted.'

Jo was sat to Tony's right in a plastic chair. Laney was sat opposite Tony, on the far side of their table. Nick was sat to Tony's left. Fred was curled up under the table like a pet.

'Woof woof,' said Fred.

'Come on, Tony, drink.'

'Woof,' said Tony, drinking.

'You alright, love?' said Laney, not looking at him, but looking over to the stage now the piano had sprung to life.

'She's not really going to play that thing is she?' said Nick.

'Why not?' said Jo.

The pianist broke into a rhythm – *oom cha cha, oom cha cha.*

'She's playing a bloody waltz, Mum,' said Nick. 'What do you think of that?'

Laney looked away from Nick.

'You alright, Tony?' said Jo.

Tony didn't answer but watched as figures began to stand from chairs and tables in the darkness on all sides of the room. These figures, Tony saw, were all older people, but sprightly in their movements, most of them, heading towards the brightly lit wooden dance floor.

The trumpets slid in gently next to the piano, playing together a short clear tune as more dapper older people converged on the dance floor, hair sprayed and patted, cuffs ironed. Their shoes shone and single figures became dancing couples as – *oom cha cha* – they started to waltz.

'Waste of ivory,' said Nick. 'Don't you think, Mum? Elephants died for that.'

'Dog needs a poo,' said Fred.

'I want to dance,' said Tony, leaping up. 'Laney?' Tony held out his hand.

'Give over,' said Laney. 'You fell over in the bloody road five minutes ago.'

'I were hot. I were thirsty.'

He grabbed a glass of water off the table, gulped it down. 'It's cool in here.'

'So many wrong notes, Mum,' said Nick. 'Her eyes, I'll bet she can't see. But you don't just need to be blind to play the piano in a Stevie Wonder tribute act, you need to be able to play the piano as well.'

'You've perked up, snob,' said Jo.

'I want to dance, Laney.'

'It's a massive one. A big smelly one.'

'I don't think calling for a basic familiarity with an instrument is snobbery.'

'Give over, Tony,' said Laney.

'Come on, dance with me.'

'You've got sun stroke.'

'Dance with me, Laney.'

'I'll dance with you,' said Jo, standing up and offering Tony her hand.

'Right then,' said Tony, taking it.

Tony turned. He could feel Laney's eyes on him as he walked away with Jo, picking their way round tables and chairs and headed towards the dance floor. In front of them a wizened man in a pressed blue safari suit danced with a lady in pearls and a sundress, a dainty white cardie draping her shoulders. Tony and Jo made the dance floor and found a space. He turned to face her. Jo took his left hand in her right, raised it and put her right hand on his shoulder.

Oom cha cha. They started to move.

'You okay, Tony?' she asked.

'Me? Oh yeah. I'm dancing. Bloody Travolta, me.'

When they were close he was surprised how big her tum was, pressing against his own. 'Why are you in Spain, Jo? What are you up to?'

'Oh,' – *oom cha cha* – 'You know what I'm up to Tony.'

'Do I?'

'If you think about it you do, Tony.'

'I have thought about it. I don't know. Might I just get a little help?'

'What do you think you're getting now?'

'Why are you so pushy?' he asked.

She pushed him for an answer, pushed his belly with her own. 'Can't you see?' she said, looking down. He followed her eyes down himself, saw the bump clearly then when she shoved it out. She was pregnant. Clear as bloody day. 'Bloody hell. Nick never said.'

'Nick doesn't know.'

What? 'Why not? Are you two on the rocks or something?'

'How many kids do we have, Tony?'

'One.'

'And if we have another, how many will we have then?'

'Two. What?'

'And what day is it?'

Tony closed his eyes. 'Bugger off.' He opened them and stared at Jo. 'You're mad.'

'I might be, Tony. But we're going to sort this family together.'

She was loopy, a few beds short of an hospital. He didn't know entirely what she meant. A baby though. A bloody baby in the family was always good news. He laughed, twirled her around. 'Congratulations,' said Tony. 'I'm really happy.'

'Thanks. Good,' said Jo. 'So am I.'

'You'd better tell Nick.'

'I will.'

'When?'

'Today, Tony, right after you've said what you need to.'

The music stopped. The waltzing came to an end, the dancers waiting as the pianist and trumpeters had a murmuring chat about what to play next. Jo took Tony's hand and led him from the dance floor. She was leading him by the hand through the dark back towards the light. He noticed that he was wearing yellow espadrilles.

'Stick together or we'll lose,' Jo whispered to him. 'You and me. Stick together. We're a team now, Tony, a weird buddy movie. You got it?'

He half knew what she meant, but he half didn't too. They made the table. Jo waited until Tony sat down then she sat down herself. She jumped straight in.

'I was in her class, you know,' said Jo. 'At school.'

'What?' said Laney.

'Jo. Don't,' said Nick.

'I was in the same class as Clare.'

Laney went white soon as Jo said the name.

'Give over,' said Laney. 'You were never.'

'She were,' said Nick. 'But don't, Jo.'

Laney was staring at Jo now like her eyes were going to pop. Tony was scared for Laney. He was feeling a little wobbly himself. Jo waved her hand and suddenly a waiter was there, like she had powers or something. Tony didn't listen to what Jo ordered, he was staring at Laney who looked mad as a dog that might chomp off its tongue. The waiter went and Jo looked at Tony for a moment, then she carried on.

'There were two of us at school took it really bad. Me and Jane. We were best mates with your Clare.'

'You weren't. You can't have been.'

'I came round your house for tea, Laney.'

'You didn't.'

'She did, Mum.'

'Why don't I remember?'

'You need to ask yourself that question, Laney,' said Jo.

'Do you remember, Tony?'

'No, Laney,' said Tony.

'He was never there, Laney,' said Jo. 'Always at work weren't you, Tony. Earning a crust.'

Laney and Tony looked at each other. Laney looked desperate.

'Me and Jane,' said Jo. 'We took it really bad. It was horrible. We loved Clare.'

'You didn't.'

'Mum.'

'Nobody wanted to talk about it. The school was embarrassed, just pretending it didn't happen. And after the funeral me and Jane stopped being mates too.'

'But you didn't come to the funeral,' said Laney. 'I'd have known if you'd have come to the funeral.'

'No, I didn't come. We weren't invited. School wasn't told when...
Her best mates. You lot were so into your own grief it never occurred
to you that her friends might be suffering too.'

'But...' said Laney.

'Or that we might be able to help you,' said Jo.

'Is this right, Nick?' asked Tony.

'It is.'

'Bloody hell,' said Tony. 'I'm sorry. Wish you'd have come. I never
knew. I'm sorry.'

'You're alright Tony. Not your fault. And not your fault how
she died either.'

'Eh!' said Laney. 'You stay out of that.'

Jo reared up, her voice breaking at the edges. 'You're not the
only people who loved her. You're not the only people who lost
her. And you can't tell me to stay out of something I'm already
in.'

The waiter arrived. He put four large brandies on the table, and
a bowl of strawberry ice cream. Jo passed the ice cream under the
table.

'None of this is right,' said Laney.

Jo looked like she was going to speak but then she said nothing.

'You're torturing us,' said Laney.

Jo looked over to Tony and he knew he had to do it: in for a
penny, in for a pound.

'The pub is thirty grand in debt, Laney.'

'What?'

'Viva. It's knackered, been losing money for three years now. I
clean pools to get some coin in, Laney. Most of the pools on our
road, as you'd have noticed if you took your eyes off the bloody sun
for a moment.'

Laney stared at Tony, then looked quickly over to Jo. 'What is
this?' she said. 'What are you two doing?'

'I get twenty quid a month each pool I do, that's what's keeping
us afloat.'

'Bollocks,' said Laney. 'We're alright for money.'

'Bollocks!' shouted Fred.

'When were the last time you had a look, Laney? You're like some big kid.'

Laney wouldn't look at Tony now.

'I'm knackered, Laney, I'm exhausted. I can't keep it in anymore.'

Laney grabbed at her brandy, quickly drank it. 'Keep what in?' she said gravely.

'The truth. You're not ill. You haven't got SAD.'

'What?'

'You've made it up. We all prefer the sun to the bloody rain, Laney, but there's no need to talk it up into some condition so you can get out of going home.'

Laney glared at him quickly and with contempt then turned away again.

'Yes, *home*. Home. The village where we used to live. The village where Clare's buried.'

'Stop it.'

'Why won't you talk about her, Laney? She were so lovely and I want to talk about her.'

'So we can fight.'

'I miss her. I want her photos in our house.'

'Stop it, Tony.'

'Hiding in the valley won't make it go away. There's no shadows to hide in in the sun.'

'Stop it.'

'I'm killing myself to keep us afloat. You've made up some illness to hide in.'

A new brandy was put down in front of Tony and he knocked it back. 'The truth is, Laney Metcalfe, that I've always loved you more than you've loved me and I've indulged you and pampered you and I've let you get away with murder.'

'*You've* let *me* . . .' started Laney, but then stopped dead.

'I want to go home and see her grave.'

'Nobody's stopping you,' Laney said.

'I want to go with you.'

Something loomed up to the left of Tony's vision. It was Nick, standing up. Tony'd forgotten that Nick was even there. 'Seems like business as usual.'

'Hardly, Nick,' said Jo.

'No, you don't get my meaning. It's these two, still caught up. It were years ago that she died and these two are still lugging it around like a sack of shit, some ghost in the house, a migraine we all share.'

'Oh Christ, Nick,' said Laney. 'Very dramatic.'

'Piss off, Mum.'

'Piss!'

'You've always been more interested in your dead kid than your living one.'

'Bloody hell, Nick,' said Tony jumping to his feet, 'Son. Son.'

But Nick had turned already and was moving away from the table, walking towards the bright rectangle of sunlight, and the waves and shore beyond.

'Nick, you can't go, Jo's…' shouted Tony, just catching himself in time.

Nick turned then, but not because of what Tony had said. He turned and looked dead straight at Jo. 'You know how you're always going on about wanting a family. Well have mine, I'm done with them.' Nick turned again and walked towards the light.

Tony looked at Nick. *Tell him, Jo*, he thought. *Tell him.*

'Nick,' Jo said to Nick's back, her voice clear and simple. 'I'm pregnant.'

'Pregnant!' shouted Fred from under the table.

Nick stopped dead, his legs and his head all still suddenly. He looked like he was going to turn back to face them, but then he started to walk away again, towards the pavement and the sunlight, and nobody followed.

SQUARE

TONY

Tony knocked and it was Laddo that opened the door, his glasses dead wonky. He looked at Tony. He didn't seem chuffed to see him.

'Brought you these,' said Tony, curling his right arm out from behind his back to show a bunch of flowers. 'Sorry,' said Tony.

'You tit,' said Laddo. 'What you being mean for?'

'I know. Sorry. There were things going on.'

'We know,' said Shirl appearing behind Laddo in the cool of the villa. 'Problems at home.' She spotted the flowers. 'They for me?'

'They are,' said Tony, reaching across the threshold and handing them to Shirl.

'You'd better come in,' she said. 'Budge over, Laddo.'

But Laddo didn't budge. 'Where's *my* present?' he said. 'What am I? Chopped bloody liver?'

Tony reached into his pocket, pulled out a little square of card, handed it to Laddo.

'What's this?'

'Read it,' said Tony.

'*Grand Opening.*'

'You've already re-opened,' said Shirl. 'Done that new menu at least. Why don't you just stay open instead of opening and re-opening?'

'We're doing it properly. That's a free ticket, everything on the house all night.'

'One for the tight bastards, eh Tony?'

'I don't mean that.'

'No, you're alright. Only messing. Thanks for this. When is it?'

'Tomorrow.'

'Great.'

'One thing.'

They eyed Tony suspiciously.

'We need you, Shirl.'

'Oh right, now we get to it. Flowers and tickets to butter us up,' said Laddo, all cross again.

Tony said nothing.

Shirl stepped out of the shadows and moved to stand at the side of Laddo. 'What is it?'

Tony told her.

Shirl laughed. 'Blimey,' she said. 'Not sure. Bit rusty.'

There was a long strip of wood laid out in the shade by the broken fountain in the middle of the square. There was a village girl, Maria, one of the mullets from the village band that hung out by the dry fountain, she was leant over the strip of wood, painting it.

Tony approached her, squinting over her shoulder to see what she was up to.

Dab hand she was, this Maria. Tony rated her. Jo had hired her for a few days to help out.

'*Bueno*,' said Tony, pointing at the sign.

'*Gracias*,' said the girl, carrying on painting.

Jo came up behind Tony. 'Pretty good, eh?'

Tony turned and looked at Jo. Over her shoulder was slung a great big bag full of the fliers she'd designed and had printed. Her stomach stuck out now she'd ditched the purdah of her cardie. She was stood in the sun, ready to go. He could tell she was a bit shaken about Nick walking out, but she wasn't exactly one to lie down and surrender to circumstance.

'Any word?' asked Tony.

'Got this,' said Jo. She showed Tony her phone. A text from Nick.

Need time. Kiss to Fred.

'Well that's something.'

'It's something,' said Jo. 'But it's not the right thing.'

'Where do you think he is?'

'Are there any bars in Spain, Tony?'

'One or two.'

'Well, that's where he'll be.'

They both looked over at the girl Maria, still painting the wood in the square.

'Looks good,' said Jo.

'Smashing,' said Tony. 'Tremendous.'

'How's Laney?'

'Hiding. She climbs in the wardrobe when I come home.'

'What?'

'I'm joking. She's hiding her feelings. She's in, what they call it, denial.'

'Stick together,' Jo said seriously. 'Straighten you all out.'

Tony frowned. 'That's why you came out, Jo, to straighten out us daft Metcalfes?'

Jo paused, looked Tony in the eye. But she didn't say anything.

'Laney says you're a meddling cow.'

'Laney might be right.'

'And what about you, Jo? You straight already?'

'Oh Tony, don't you know?'

'Don't I know what?'

'I don't count.'

'You don't count?' Tony frowned again. 'How come?'

But she didn't answer. 'Right,' said Jo, holding up a flier taken from her bag. 'I've got to deliver these. Our village today, rest of the valley next week.'

'You sure I can't...?'

'We need you making phone calls. I'm pregnant, not crippled.'

Jo walked slowly towards the house next to Viva and shoved a flier through the letterbox. Tony watched her. 'Nick will come back when he's ready, Jo.'

'He'll come before that.'

'What?'

'I've cancelled his cards, told the bank they've been stolen.'

'Never!'

'Severed his supply lines.'

'Christ.'

'Pretty good, eh Tony.'

'I'm glad you're on my side, Jo.'

'Oh we're on the same side, Tony, long as you do what you should.'

Tony watched as Jo started moving down the shaded side of the street, pushing a flier into one letterbox, then one in the next.

NICK

It was only afternoon, but Nick had been drinking since late morning and he was already plastered. He turned to the stag night, taking in the Viking helmets, the fairy wings, the stuck-on moustaches. '*Hombres*,' Nick said. 'My round.'

A Viking cheered and clattered his football studs. Another raised his Stetson. The groom clapped some giant latex testicles against a bar stool. The air was sticky. Almost every wall wore a plasma screen. Nick shoved his elbows across the bar, waving his plastic at the barman of Lineker's, the premier football bar and grill in Benidorm.

The barman was called Geezer; Nick knew this from the lettering on his knuckles and throat. 'For you, Rocky Balboa,' said Geezer. 'It's on the house.'

Nick had just become a hero in the bar after burping the theme to *Rocky*.

He knocked back the drink. It landed a heavy punch. Nick slumped off his chair, fell backwards and slammed down onto the bar-room floor. His eyes closed as he hit the tiles. The stag night cheered and sang. Nick lay flat out on the floor tiles and groaned.

'Rocky is down,' said the stag night.

Nick opened his eyes and peered and looked along his prone body. He was wearing football boots. A dark forest of ankles moved around his head. A peanut dropped down from one of the drinkers above him and bounced off his eye.

'Rocky! Rocky! Rocky!' bellowed the stag night.

Nick turned his head and looked through the ankles towards the bar window. Out of the window, from where he lay on the tiles, the sky seemed huge and the sun made him squint even through the dark glass. A bus stopped at the pavement right in front of the bar. Nick looked up from the floor to the bus. A figure waited at the bus stop, a young girl.

He sat up. His head banged like hell. Nick slowly stood.

'Rocky's beaten the count,' a Viking said.

Nick scrambled to his feet and walked over to the window. He watched the girl step onto the bus and disappear inside. Nick watched the doors shut and the bus drive away.

TONY

He was dreading this call most of all. Tony was sat behind the bar. He had his little phone book out, and a pen and a paper next to it. He made himself do it – he picked up the phone and dialled.

'Hello, Fon...' Tony said, nearly blowing it. 'Hello Brian.'

'Who's that?'

'Tony Metcalfe.'

'Ah, Tony! How's your dated little pub?'

'Good.'

'Right... Penny, it's Tony on the phone, terrible line, sounds like he's calling from the past.'

Tony bit his lip, then said, 'Brian I'd love you to come tomorrow night. We're relaunching Viva. It's a private thing.' Tony felt sick for talking this flannel. 'Friends and family only, to start with, you know.'

'Friends and family? I...'

'*Arròs negra* is on the menu.'

'Really?'

'We've got a new chef.'

'Oh.'

'Spanish.'

'Really?'

'See you both there I hope.'

'Well I think you just might,' Font purred.

Tony hung up. What a closet that Font was – an utter specimen. What a prize-winning shit-house. Tony felt weird. It wasn't in his nature to phone anyone – he'd been a reluctant receiver of incoming calls all his life – let alone flatter and smarm while he was on the line. He never did that, never put himself forward, never made a song and dance about what he was up to, like some people did, and like he was now up to with this ringing round all the people he knew that were still here. But there you go. It was funny what life had you doing. The things you did when you needed to.

He heard the voice of his old mum in his head: *You're making a spectacle of yourself, Tony. Setting yourself for a fall.* But he didn't listen to that, just smiled to himself, turned again to the little phone book. There was something awake inside Tony and he was going to stick up for himself a bit. He was going to make things work.

He leafed the pages. Bev and Martin he'd called already. They'd moved back home to England. Kat and Pieter the German couple, he'd called them too. They were coming. What about Marja and Claes, the Dutchies they'd met years ago? Maybe they were still around and would be glad of it. He picked up the phone. Tony started dialling then heard a noise and looked over to the pub entrance. It was Pepe, popping his head in.

'What is this?' Pepe asked, smiling.

Pepe meant the two ladders on the pavement outside.

Tony put his pencil down and walked round the bar towards Pepe. They shook hands in the doorway then stepped outside, taking a few paces backwards into the square and looking up, shielding their eyes from the sun. There was a ladder either side of the pub entrance, and up each ladder there was a local lass. Maria was up one, and her mate, Rosa, the other mullet in the village band, she was up the other. Maria and Rosa both had belts on with hammers jammed into them, and they both had a little battery drill bulging a pocket of their cargo pants. They were stepping carefully up towards the top of the ladders, holding something between them across the gap. It was the long strip of wood that Maria had painted.

When they got up high they flipped the wood around, so that the painted side was now facing outwards and they handled the wood so that it lay flush against the old *Viva España* sign. Tony peered upwards as Rosa and Maria clonked a big nail into each end of the new sign to hold it in place, then Maria reached for the drill and started pushing screws in, to really stick it down, and Rosa did the same.

'Tony.' Pepe grabbed Tony and kissed him on top of the head. 'I love it.'

Home Sweet Home, the new sign read.

Pepe laughed. 'Does this mean you have given in Tony, accepted what your life has long been telling you, that Spain is now your home sweet home?'

'Have I chuff. I'm Yorkshire born and bred. Just vamping up the pub to flog it. Going to be nabbing quite a few customers from you, Pepe,' said Tony, 'over the next few weeks.'

'Excellent, excellent,' said Pepe, clapping his hands together. 'Take all my customers. Have them. They are lazy and dirty. Many of them are bastards.'

Tony laughed. The church bells rang. Pepe smiled. He looked up. Maria and Rosa had finished screwing the sign into place and they were climbing down the ladders, chatting away to each other. The village girls walked inside, ready for the next job.

Tony said, 'No chance yet with Lita? About moving?'

Pepe sighed. 'You know, maybe there is, maybe a chink of light. She was talking about Venice the other day, she was talking about Crete.'

'She wants to go?'

'Maybe... We see. But this is a funny situation, Tony, you think?'

'What?'

Pepe gestured up towards the new sign. 'Home. Us. Our predicament. You, Tony are away from home, trying to get back. And me, Pepe, I am at home trying to get away.'

'Seems daft.'

'Yes, daft, Tony. We are a couple of pillocks, is this the right English?'

'Yes, *pillocks*. Good word. We are pillocks. A bit pillocky. You could say that. Or you could say we were wazzocks.'

'Wazzocks,' said Pepe. 'I like it. Very good word. Feels quick in your mouth. Jumps out. Wazzocks... But are we closets, Tony?' asked Pepe. 'Could we say we are closets?'

'We could,' said Tony. 'We could say we are closets. A right pair of closets.'

'Excellent. What of bollocks?' Pepe tried. 'Are we bollocks?'

'Well, no, I wouldn't say we were bollocks.'

'Okay,' said Pepe. 'We are not bollocks. But we are wazzocks and closets.'

'Yes, Pepe. And pillocks.'

'Yes, we are pillocks.'

They stood a little closer together and looked up to the new sign.

Tony thought about the relaunch. 'Are you and Lita coming over tomorrow?'

'Of course, my friend,' said Pepe gently. 'Of course we are.'

There is a small category of people who wear bandanas but are not closets, and the new chef Luis sneaked into that category, just. He was the kind of chef who brought his own, better oven gloves to a new kitchen. He was precise, organised, more than a little cranky and ever so slightly up himself. Luis was quickly sliding hot trays of canapés out from the oven and serving the food out onto platters, where he straightened them and fussed over them and would have plumped them too, perhaps, if he could.

Tony was watching in the kitchen doorway. He looked from busy Luis over towards Shirl.

Shirl was petrified, hiding right at the back of the kitchen by the open back door. She was clutching a piece of paper. It was a flier advertising the entertainment for the re-opening. The words were written in English on one side and written in Spanish on the other. But whichever way Shirl turned the flier, her name was still there, advertised as appearing. Shirl was playing piano at the grand reopening.

Tony walked through the hot kitchen over towards Shirl. She was looking out of the back door towards the yellow-splashed hills.

'Pissing with nerves,' said Shirl.

Tony smiled. 'You're not alone, Shirl. I'm shitting chutney.'

'*Shitting chutney*. I've never heard that. One of your granny's sayings?'

'One of my own.'

'It's good. Vivid. Are you really scared, Tony?'

'Course I am. Big night.'

'Laney coming?'

'Don't know.'

'What's got into her?'

'Long story.'

'How long?'

'Twenty-five years.'

'*Riiiight*,' said Shirl, not getting it.

'Go and have another tinkle, Shirl.'

'I've just been.' Shirl nodded towards the toilet door.

'I mean on the piano.'

'Oh. Right.' Shirl laughed. 'I can't.'

'Suit yourself,' said Tony. He walked by the new chef Luis towards one of the serving platters. 'Thanks, Luis.' Tony lifted the platter, holding it shoulder-high on his fingertips, like he'd seen a posh waiter on a film do. '*El garçon* or what,' he said to nobody in particular.

Tony emerged from the kitchen with the proudly hoisted tray.

Jo was quiet behind the bar. She was laying cava flutes out ready to pour.

Tony put the tray down expertly and looked round the pub. A lick of paint had cheered it up and the nautical memorabilia had gone. The place seemed clean and open and ready. The place looked good. Apart from being completely empty. Because not a soul had come.

Tony wasn't going to panic though. Well he was, but he wasn't going to show it.

Maria and Rosa clattered in from the square with their instrument cases.

'Shirl! They're here!' Tony shouted back into the kitchen.

The girls smiled at Tony and walked towards the back of the pub, putting their cases down on a small raised platform. It was a stage, and the girls had sawn the wood and screwed it together themselves. They'd cleared the space in front of the stage too and laid a small wooden dance floor. The pub's old piano, once dusty and pushed aside, now sat on the stage and shone with polish and elbow grease. Maria and Rosa climbed on the stage and opened their cases, taking out their trumpets.

'Shirl!' Tony called. 'Come out.'

And Shirl came out, a little hesitant at first, but as she got closer to the girls a big smile cracked out of her. Maria took out her trumpet and Rosa did the same and then Shirl stepped onto the stage and sat down smiling on the stool in front of the piano.

'Right then,' Shirl said, all nerves gone, and began to jab out some practice notes.

The trumpets started parping a bit too, in a warming-up sort of way, and Tony saw from the corner of his eye the door open and Laddo come in. Good. Right. That was a start. It was a mate, come to see his wife and for a free piss-up, but at least it was one.

And one was one up from none.

The door opened again. Consuela with the huge hennaed hair bustled in then Gabriel the sleepy mayor sloped in afterwards. Excellent. That was two more. Tony rubbed his hands together a little. Consuela and Gabriel had never set foot in here before, had never graced the expat pub.

Tony walked over. 'Hello. Welcome.'

They both looked past Tony, waving to Maria on the stage.

'*Mamá. Papá,*' called Maria, waving back.

Tony felt squashed. They'd only come in to support their daughter Maria. But still. It was something that they were even inside.

Consuela reached the bar. '*Dos canea,*' she said to Jo.

'*Mui bien,*' said Jo quietly, lifting the beer glasses.

Tony watched Gabriel peer around the pub, into the ceiling corners and into the corners on the floor.

'You have spiders?' Consuela asked Jo.

'No spiders,' said Jo. '*No hay arañas,*' she repeated, towards Gabriel.

Gabriel nodded and walked to the bar. He rubbed a finger on top of the bar then inspected his fingertip. He held up the beer that Jo put down in front of him and he peered at that.

'My husband is a particular man,' said Consuela.

Gabriel drank his beer and then said something from the corner of his mouth.

Consuela looked at Jo. 'My husband likes you and he likes the bar and he is glad to be here and he is looking forward to the evening. He feels that this is a place where a man – in time – might untuck his trousers.'

'He said all that?' blurted Tony. 'Just then?'

'He meant it. He also asked when are you opening the cava?'

'Now,' said Tony. 'Your English is brilliant. Why didn't I know?'

'You would have done, Tony Metcalfe, if I had heard you speak more Spanish.'

Tony was surprised at the use of his full name and his face must have shown it.

'Everyone in the valley knows the Metcalfe *por favors.*'

'*Por favors?*'

'An expatriate with no Spanish. Or only enough Spanish to ask for the toilet.'

'Right.' Tony looked a bit glum. 'Sorry about the Spanish, Consuela. Must try harder.'

'It would be nice.'

Jo opened the cava and slowly poured two glasses.

'Pour it all, Jo. *Todo.* Open another. Laddo, come over here. Shirl, Rosa, Maria. *Vamos.*'

Jo handed cava to Consuela and Gabriel, then started on another bottle as everyone met at the bar. They were clinking their glasses when the door opened again and Font and Penny walked in.

Font's eyes lit up. 'Consuela. Gabriel.'

Tony could tell that Font was surprised. Consuela and Gabriel were here in Tony's expat pub. He was a closet, Font, and he had a loud, poisonous voice, but Tony was going to draw his sting. Tony picked up a tray, met Font and Penny as they walked to the bar and offered them a nibble. Then Tony turned to Laddo, and offered him a nibble too, all mock gallant.

'You tit,' said Laddo, shoving his big glasses up his nose, but he smiled at Tony and took one, his big fingers bashing into the tray. Tony was getting quite into this gliding about thing, this meet and greet. Front of house was okay. Better than kitchen maybe. Then the door rattled again. It was Marja and Claes, the Dutchies from yonks ago. They were pissed already, he could tell.

'Tony!' they both yelled, almost falling across the gap towards him.

What a laugh. It'd been years, and seeing them tanked-up with their suntans and their laughter lines and their bleached teeth, well, it made him think of the happy valley, what it was a few years ago, all the bloody fun they'd had, him and Laney and the rest, when they'd first got here, eating out most nights, getting hammered. And it looked like Claes and Marja were still on that ride.

'Yeah!' yelled Claes.

Daft as a brushes, Marja and Claes, the pair of them.

Marja reached for Tony and gave him a hug that cricked his back, then she kissed him on the lips and twirled away. Jo was popping the bubbles and people were chatting and scoffing the new chef's grub, and Claes' big teeth were grinning away as the Dutchie grabbed his old friend Tony and hugged. And Tony smiled. He hugged back, peering over Claes' cashmere shoulder to see Pepe and Lita. They were holding hands, walking across the square together towards Home Sweet Home.

The lights were low. Tony was watching from behind the bar.

Maria had finished playing her trumpet for the night and she was chatting with Luis, who still had his cooking whites on. They were drinking beers by the bar. They were good kids, they'd worked well. Tony banged the till open and looked inside.

Very good. Although the night was free for those who'd been invited, Tony had made a fair few quid too. Once the dancing had got going, and once she'd got filled with local cava, Consuela had started working at her mobile, getting her pals in the village to come down. Quite a few had come – they were just leaving now – and while Tony had watered them for nothing to show he was willing, they'd also ordered quite a bit of grub. It was much higher takings than for a normal night anyway. It was a fine start. He was on the march, a firm first step on the road back home. His accountant Chitta had told him weeks ago that he couldn't hope to sell a failing pub, especially with Brexit on the horizon. Well, things were different now. There was new wind in his sails. He looked proudly at the notes in the till – many of them from Spanish – then picked up his mobile and texted Chitta.

Come to pub for lunch. Tony wrote. *Won't recognise place.*

Tony put his phone down and looked over to see Font and Penny were leaving the pub.

'See you again.' said Tony, waving.

'You certainly will,' said Penny.

Tony watched them out, then he took more notes from the till. He split those notes in two and handed half over the bar to Maria, then the other half to Luis. They pocketed their notes, barely breaking their chat, like they'd been working there for years. He liked that. He looked round. Consuela was still there, spraffling away to Laddo, with Gabriel asleep in a chair, one sock slightly untucked from a hitched-up trouser. From the small stage, Shirl and Rosa played a sleepy waltz, their *oom cha chas* yawningly slow.

Four people danced.

Claes and Marja moved slowly, coming to a complete stop at times, propping each other up like playing cards. Pepe and Lita were in the middle of the floor. Pepe was holding Lita's hand and kissing her forehead as they turned slowly round. The night had melted them together.

Tony pulled some more notes from the till. Those were for Jo. He looked around the room but couldn't see her. But he did see something.

A man outside, a short man carrying a brown leather briefcase. The short stranger was standing on his own in the moonlit square, peering into the darkness of Pepe's long-closed bar. He seemed to be scanning Pepe's for signs of life. But there were none and the man then did a half turn and began to peer across to Tony's bar, his face now lit by the husky, late-night lights of Home Sweet Home.

Tony pocketed the notes he had for Jo and closed the till. He walked over and stepped into the kitchen and there she was, out the back on her mobile.

'*I* cancelled the cards,' Jo said into her phone. 'It was me.'

Tony handed Jo her cash, 'Thanks,' she said to Tony. 'No, not you,' she said into the phone. 'Thanks to your dad.' Her voice lowered, 'You sound close, Nick…. We need you back.'

Tony turned to walk away, but, 'He's hung up,' said Jo. 'He said not to call again.'

Tony turned back.

'Stubborn bastard,' said Jo.

'Unlike us,' Tony said. 'Push us over with a hanky.'

'I didn't expect him to disappear like this, Tony. I didn't plan for that to happen.'

She looked so tired. He gave her a cuddle. 'He'll come round, Jo. He's a good lad.'

But Tony wasn't so sure. He used to be a good lad, but bad things made bad people and bad things had happened to Nick. Life was corrupting. Life was insidious. Some people couldn't take it.

Tony stepped out of the kitchen and across the pub and out of the door and outside into the night. The air was clean as soap. Across the square, the short stranger with the brown leather briefcase was climbing into an old saloon car. Tony stood on the pavement and listened to the car's engine cough to life. The car rattled away down a slender road and away from the village and Tony stood quietly until the sound of the stranger's car had long gone.

Tony breathed deeply. The square was quiet and still. The night was warm and soft and the moon sailed high above the church. He sensed a movement and his eyes moved down. Then he saw it. In the shadow that hemmed the church there stood a figure. An outline of a figure he knew well. He knew she'd have to come and have a peek. He squinted towards the dark figure. She was babysitting, so she had Fred next to her sleeping in the buggy.

Tony wanted to call out to Laney but he didn't. Still, he was glad she'd come.

He stepped back towards the pub and opened the door and propped it open, so the gentle music could come out into the square and Laney could hear it and remember, he hoped, the last time they had danced. Tony looked back across the square. His eyes found her in the shadow. He saw her in the dark like an animal sees its mate.

He wanted to walk over and hold her but now it was up to her to walk to him.

He loved that lass like anything but she had to come round.

LANEY

Laney looked at her husband Tony, standing in the lights that came out from the pub. He was quite far off but she'd know the shape of him anywhere; whatever clothes you stuck on him he made them look scruffy, he was like some cloth-eared poodle, like some ratty old toy. He might be able to see her. She could see him plain as day. But then Tony was standing in the light from the bar and she was standing in the shadows, so she couldn't be sure.

She hoped Tony couldn't see her, hoped that she'd not been caught spying.

Laney was aiming to seem aloof to Tony's schemes. There was no gain in reacting to what he was doing. It'd fizzle out sooner or later. The valley sent everything to sleep in the end, didn't it? Wasn't that the point of being there?

She peered at Tony standing alone outside the bar. What was he doing? Popped out to pick his nose? She nearly laughed. He wasn't moving, just looking towards the place where she was. She looked beyond Tony towards Viva behind him, or Home Sweet Home as he now reckoned.

Husky orange lights from the pub let her see inside.

Laney watched Pepe and Lita dance. They'd been at it like that – turning slowly round – since she'd got to her spying place by the church. Dancing near Pepe and Lita was another couple, the mad Dutchies that her and Tony had known yonks back. What were they doing there? And what about all them Spanish from the village, and Font and Penny who'd been in too? Laney had seen them all troop out. They didn't normally come in the pub. The place seemed almost busy, and she couldn't have that.

But it wouldn't last. He'd not keep at it. She'd stay quiet and mardy and he'd come back to her. That was the way their marriage had always worked. She went quiet and got what she wanted. Her silence was their bloody anchor. Tony would be back to being Easy Tony in a bit. Though even as she thought that she knew that it was wrong and that Tony had changed and Easy Tony had gone, and that this New Tony was intent on dredging things up, making her say the things she did not want to say.

Laney peered into Home Sweet Home.

She saw meddling Jo walk slowly out from the kitchen doorway to stand quiet behind the bar, where Laney used to be when they first opened, before she'd given up really, before she'd given in to the heat of the valley, its colours that send you barking – the blue of the pool winking at the blue of the sky and the greens between in clean swipes of pine. Just lying there below the hill: sunlounger, a few thick books on the go, dragon flies diving down to drink from the pool and more bloody booze than you could even see. A year might flit like that. You could wish ten away.

What right had Jo to turn up here and start shoving everybody about, shake them all from sleep?

From inside the pub Laney could hear the piano and the trumpet still playing, a hobbly *oom cha cha*, so feint it was barely making it out the door. Through the window, Laney could see Rosa the village girl standing on a stage playing the trumpet, with Shirl alongside on the piano.

Even her mate Shirl was in there helping. It felt like they were ganging up.

Laney heard another sound, gentle, like a bird. What was it? She looked over. It was Tony still stood outside in light, now whistling along to the waltz coming out from the pub. Trying to anyway, thinking he was tuneful.

He was looking right at her. Or looking at where she was.

She looked at Tony across the square. He seemed to be moving, swaying slightly as he whistled, like he was dancing. Daft beggar was cracking up.

She remembered the last time she'd danced with him, in England all those years ago.

NICK

Nick stood unseen in the square. His dad stood in the light and his mum stood in the shadow with his son sleeping by her in the pushchair. Nick could see pregnant Jo, still behind the bar. For once she couldn't see him but he could see her. Usually he felt that she was scrutinising him, peering right in, whereas he couldn't see into her at all. Her eyes were a one-way mirror. She looked all the time at others so as not to be looked at herself.

Moonlight blotted out stars and made the night simple.

Nick was glugging from a bottle. He was looking towards the pushchair standing next to Laney. He'd love to see Fred's face. He almost could. The chair was facing towards Nick, but shadows fell across it, too dark.

He had another drink. Nick wasn't ready to come back. Not yet. He was dossing in some rustic hotel in the next village, parsing out the money he'd whipped out as his cards went down. The night seemed uncanny to him. Nick looked across the square. Tony was on his left side, Laney was by the church on his right. He himself took a third side.

Nick looked to the empty fourth side of the square.

Except it wasn't empty, was it? Whenever there was three of them there was always really four of them. Clare was the fourth, his sister, eight years old, always the fourth in the same green dress she died in.

He had found her. Clare missing and everyone scouring the village but it was Nick her brother that knew her favourite places, and it was Nick that had jumped the wall at the back of the garden and sprinted down the hill into the field and across to the river, and it was Nick who had seen her churning in the weir, face down, hair sea-weeded out long behind. She was barefoot, one of her shoes caught in the circular tumble of flood, turning round in the water with her, and Clare's other shoe – Nick looked down – placed neatly on the grass, a neat ankle sock placed neatly inside.

He'd shouted then, screamed. Like a heel had stamped on his heart.

And he'd gone on screaming since, though mostly in his head, mostly into the bottle, sometimes silenced by Jo. He had a drink. Nick had played piano with Clare the day before she'd died. The prodigy Nick was supposed to be teaching her to play but they'd only ever plink and plonk about in the old front room. *The good room* as they called it, *The Sunday Room* even, Nick had once heard an auntie say. It was the early 1990s but his village was a pocket of time all its own.

It was Monday, high summer, windows open. Nick was sixteen. Clare was eight. She was in the dress she would die in. The piano stool in the good room was long enough for them both to perch and Nick was working the peddles as they clonked at the keyboard.

'*Row, row, row,*' sang little Clare, and Nick joined in.

'No, silly pants,' she said. 'I sing the first line *then* you do.'

He knew that. He'd just wanted to sing with her. She had good pitch.

'*Row row row your boat,*' sang Clare.

'*Gently down the stream,*' sang Clare, as Nick sang, '*Row row row your boat.*'

'*Merrily, merrily, merrily, merrily,*' sang Clare, with Nick following her a line behind.

'*Life is but a dream.*'

They started again, then, '*Row row row your boat,*' Laney sang, stepping into the front room with her apron on. '*Gently down the stream,*' Laney sang, her voice flat as a pancake, but she had a smile on her face for once, and then there was a noise outside and Tony's biffed-up work car stopped by the pavement and Tony himself was peering out the driver's window to spy them all by the piano. And Tony was out the car quick-sharp. He was smiling and because of the open window, he'd joined in the singing before he'd even got into the house. And then he was through the front door and up the hall like a shot, and the four of them stood in the front room and sang a song, all together, each one saying the same words at different times.

It was brilliant. The family was working right.

Then Tony said, 'Dance with me Laney,' and took her hand.

Nick started to play a waltz for them but Laney said, 'No, Tony. You know I don't like it.'

But, 'Yes, you do,' said bossy little Clare. 'You're just a big scaredy cat.'

Then although it was summer, and not late at all in the day, little Clare had got up and tugged the curtains shut because she knew her mum Laney would be shy of people seeing in from the street. So Laney took Tony's hand and they danced and danced slowly around the room, Nick and Clare plonking out the *oom cha chas* for them to follow, and his mum and dad whirling round a room that was curtained in summer, but just then more than ever was precisely full of love.

One night later Clare was gone.

Nick opened his eyes.

Clare was gone too from the square; the little ghost that took their happiness, left each of them standing alone. His mum was still in the square, looking across towards Home Sweet Home. But now Tony's whistling had stopped and Tony wasn't stood there anymore. He was going back inside. He stepped into the pub. The sound of the music cut dead when the door shut behind him. Nick watched his dad disappear into the bar, then he drank from his bottle and turned his head and looked across the square to the church. Laney still stood there. Fred by her side.

Nick needed to see Fred, but he couldn't face his family yet.

He pulled out his phone, wrote a message.

Hi Mum, Tell Jo I'm safe. Love to Fred. Nick x

Nick heard a little ding from across the square and saw Laney reach into her pocket. As she read the text, the light from her phone shone on little Fred's sleeping face. Nick saw his boy. The scream inside grew quieter.

BOLLOCKS

JO

Next day, Jo was dashing down to the villa.

She was hot and panting. She slipped round the back of the building.

'Laney,' called Jo, spotting her in the pool.

'Oh,' Laney said. 'It's you.'

Christ, the attitude on her, but Jo let it go. She moved on to why she'd rushed straight down. 'Tony said Nick texted you last night.'

'He did text me,' Laney said between strokes.

'Right. Okay. So what did Nick say?'

'Oh you know, *love to Fred* type-thing.'

'Okay. Anything else?'

'Nick *is* allowed to text his mother.'

Christ. 'Did he say anything else?'

'Like what?'

'That he was dying in the road with an eyeball hanging out. That his arm was severed.'

'He said he was safe.'

'Right. He's safe. Good. Did he mention me, Laney?'

'Not sure. Don't remember.'

'You're *not sure.* You *don't remember.* I'm not asking you to memorise the Koran. Did Nick mention me?'

'Can't remember.'

'Can I see the text?'

'I deleted it.'

'You deleted it? The father of my unborn child goes missing and you delete his text?'

Jo stopped herself from saying more. She turned away, stared at the sky.

This whole thing was harder than she'd thought. Yes, Tony was making progress, pushing his problems up into the day, swimming away from his sinking ship, but Nick was missing, probably fallen into a bottle, and Laney, well:

Yes my daughter died tragically but I really don't need to talk about it – not with you, or my son, or my husband, or anyone. And no, I don't want to hear her name, and no, I don't want to see her photo, and no, I don't even want to visit the country where she died, and yes I think this is healthy and normal and it has in no way caused me to be depressed, or cracked my marriage, or destroyed my son. None of those things are true, so if you could just step out of my bloody sunshine…

Jo had been wrong to start all this.

Laney would never budge. Nick would never want the baby.

Jo was sweating and suffering. What was she going to do? Her head was swimming. Tears itched at the corners of her eyes. Why did she think it could work? She should have left things hidden and broken, kept the barriers up.

Jo heard the water move as Laney turned and started another length. Jo turned on her heel and walked slowly away from the villa.

TONY

The fishmonger slapped his palm down hard on the flank of the fish to show that it was fresh.

'*Luis*! *Pesce*!' Tony bellowed through to the kitchen.

The fishmonger lifted another polystyrene box onto the bar and opened it. Patches of fish showed through the crushed ice. Luis came out to look. It was the lull before the evening rush. Tony picked his coffee off the bar and peered across the village square, beyond the shaded fountain and over to Pepe's bar which was closed and gloomy.

Tony sipped his coffee and watched as Pepe rattled up into the square in his big yellow car. Tony watched Pepe walk from the car to the door of his bar, where he stood, working his way through a big fob of keys, grumbling, shoving at the latch. Tony picked up his phone and called Pepe. He watched Pepe rifle through his pockets for his phone.

'Tony.'

'You'd have been inside by now if some bugger hadn't called you.'

'What?'

'I'm stood here watching you rattle that fob of keys like you've never been in before.'

Pepe turned round so that he faced Home Sweet Home and he waved towards the place where he knew Tony was watching. 'Big hangover,' Pepe said.

'Right,' said Tony. 'Go anywhere nice?'

'At home. Just with Lita and me, celebrating.'

'Oh right,' said Tony. 'Hang on.' There was somebody else trying to call him.

Tony checked. It was Chitta.

'I've never done this before, Pepe,' Tony said, 'but hang on, Mr Swish here has someone calling on the other line.'

Tony jabbed at his mobile in a way he hoped told it that he wanted to change lines.

It worked.

'Chitta!' Tony said. 'On line number two. I am receiving you!'

'Hi, Tony,' said Chitta. 'You called me, again.'

'Look, come and see it. It's not the same place.'

'I am not hopeful, Tony,' said Chitta.

He wasn't having that. 'There'll be a good few quid in it for you when you sell it.'

'I don't know any buyers, Tony.'

'You know buyers, Chitta. If what's been offered is right.'

'Exactly. The offer is not a good one.'

'Come and have a look at the books. You won't recognise them.'

'One lucky week, Tony.'

The door rattled. It was Consuela and her Spanish mates. They'd become a bit of a fixture.

'*Ola*, Tony! *Ola*, Luis!' Consuela called, loud enough for Chitta to hear, especially because Tony was holding the phone out to give her the best possible chance of doing so.

'See,' Tony told Chitta. 'Not just expats. Come and see.'

Tony looked out across the square, seeing Pepe now entering his bar. Tony flicked back over to line one. '*Buenas*, Consuela,' he said into the bar, loud enough for Pepe to hear.

Chitta was in the window of the pub, interrogating Tony's account book.

Every now and then Chitta would move, she would cough or twitch an arm about, and it made Tony – who was watching her like a hawk – flinch and worry. And when Chitta actually did look up, then Tony had to look away quickly, pretend he wasn't watching, wasn't trying to judge from her face what she made of his numbers. Instead Tony looked over towards Jo. She was standing still, not touching the herd of dirty glasses on the bar top, staring sadly off into a corner behind the bar.

Usually Jo was chipping away at people, shoving them on to be better. But not today. She was as dour and dark as Nick today.

Tony walked over. 'Why don't you go and sit down?'

'Stop it,' she snapped. 'Stop doing that.'

'Doing what?'

'Over-protecting me.'

'Can't I be nice to you?' he said.

'Go and be nice to someone else,' Jo said, still staring into a corner.

Tony followed her eyes over to the next batch of fliers, hanging on a hook behind the bar.

'You're not delivering all of them,' Tony said, nodding towards the fliers sitting bagged-up and ready to go. A map of the valley sat inside the bag with the fliers, andthe villages and urbanisations that were next to target were marked with highlighter pen. It was a lot of walking to get round them all.

'Course I'm bloody delivering them,' she snapped. 'Get me out of this shit hole.'

'Oh, *shit hole* now is it?' He wouldn't flare up though. The kid must really be suffering for her to talk like this. 'I am not actually letting you deliver them,' said Tony.

'Not *letting* me?'

'It's forty bloody degrees and you're up the bloody stick.'

'Don't be a knob.'

'I'll do it, Jo.'

'You can't.'

'Why not?'

'*Because it's forty bloody degrees, and you're a clumsy old...*'

'Jo!' said Tony, stopping her before she went too far. 'Take a bloody break.'

'Mr Metcalfe,' said Chitta, walking towards Tony. 'I am finished with your accounts.'

LANEY

At dusk they were walking in the lanes, Laney and Lita. The pines clicked with insects. They came to a gap in the trees and looked across the valley.

Laney stopped in her tracks and stared at Lita. 'Never!' she said.

'I have agreed it. The house is sold.'

'But what about Pepe's?'

'We are looking for a buyer.'

'And what about...' Laney waved her hands, indicating the trees, the ground, the sky. 'What about...?'

'The valley?' Lita said. She looked down at the lane, a stripe of hard red soil studded through with pebbles. 'The valley will be here when we come back.'

Laney stooped down and picked up a pebble. 'What about your work?'

'I don't know, Laney. My sister might take the business on.'

'Can't imagine the valley without you, Lita. Like the ravens leaving the tower.'

But even if Lita had understood what Laney had meant about the ravens and the tower, she wasn't listening. She was looking across the wide valley towards the dome of the village. 'It has no bad side,' Lita said. 'Every way you look – front, back, sides – the village is perfect. If I were the first woman walking through this valley I would see that hill and I would build my village there.'

'Queen Lita.'

'Exactly.'

'Why are you going, Lita? It'll break your heart.'

'You are thinking of yourself.'

'What?'

'Life is a river, all you can do is jump in.'

'Crikey!' said Laney. 'What's got into you?'

'Last week, your daughter…'

'She's not my daughter.'

'*In-law* I was going to say, Laney, if I would be given the chance.' She looked down at the path.

'Jo helped me realise…'

'Oh right, sermons from the great one.'

'Last week, she made me realise I could leave the valley.'

'Why?'

'We sniff round our past like dogs sniff round shit.'

'She said that?' asked Laney. 'About dogs and shit?'

'She said that you are angry but will not admit it.'

'Angry! Me? Balls! About what?'

'I don't know,' Lita said. 'I did not ask. Why do *you* think?' Lita started walking again, moving along the path. 'Anyway, we are nearly there.'

Laney eyed Lita warily. 'Where?' she asked.

Lita stopped right next to the spot in the undergrowth. Laney stopped too and felt the smooth stone in her hand. Lita said nothing, just stood looking beyond Laney's secret pile of stones towards the clearing of meadow grass, wild flowers dabbing it with colour. Laney just stood. Her heart was banging and banging. The smooth stone in her hand felt as hot as her burning ears. She didn't know what to do.

'Put it on,' said Lita.

'What?' faked Laney.

'The stone. Put it on.'

Laney gulped.

'My cousin saw you here. Told me what you did.'

'Oh right,' Laney said, all huffy.

'All the *por favors* are spied on.'

'Bloody seems that way.'

'Put the stone on, Laney.'

But Laney couldn't put it on. She felt trapped, cornered, her blood was pumping.

'The thing about a pile,' Lita said, 'is knowing when it is finished.'

TONY

Now it was evening and Laddo was drunk.

'Dance with me! Dance with me, Tony!'

Laddo grabbed at Tony's arm, yanking him drunkenly round the bar before Tony had the chance to refuse. Tony thought it was funny. He just went with it, danced with Laddo.

'*Oom cha cha*,' sang Laddo, his face bleary and boozed, his big glasses nowhere near the bridge of his nose. 'Come on, Tony.'

Laddo waved up to the stage. 'Quicker, Shirl, quicker.'

Shirl just laughed, kept on playing. Tony looked around as he waltzed with Laddo. Pepe was next to him, dancing with Lita. Consuela even had Gabriel up and he was gliding round with his trousers untucked, presumably finally satisfied that the bar had no spiders. There were a load of Spanish in the corner gabbing on and waiting for the food that Luis was cooking them. Font and Penny were in the window working their way through a few plates of tapas. There were even a few holidaymakers on the pavement terrace thirsting their way through rounds of beers in the warm dusk. With Jo not working, Maria was pouring drinks like mad behind the bar. It was great.

Why shouldn't Tony muck about?

Life was a veil of tears. Why not piss about when you can?

'*Oom cha cha*,' Tony said back, grabbing harder at Laddo's hand and twirling him quicker. 'Faster, Shirl! Faster!' shouted Tony.

Laddo was really laughing then, spluttering and turning round and round, and Tony was turning too and Shirl and Rosa were playing the music quicker, and Pepe and Lita were laughing too and Tony caught his mate Pepe's eye and they were grinning at each other like a couple of daft heads.

The door opened and in Chitta walked.

She had someone with her, a short man carrying a brown leather briefcase. Tony knew he'd seen the man before. Chitta led the short man into the pub and sat down with him on a window table behind Font and Penny. Tony was still being lolloped around by Laddo but he had one eye on Chitta and this bloke now too. The bloke looked out through the glass, across the dusky square towards Pepe's, then he looked back into the pub as Chitta kept talking to him. Tony had stopped dancing now. He stood still.

'Dance, Tony!' bellowed boozy Laddo. 'Dance.'

But Tony wasn't doing that now. Tony watched Maria walk from behind the bar and make to go over to serve Chitta, but, 'I'll go,' Tony said to Maria as he set off.

'Chitta, hello,' Tony said as he made the table.

'Tony, this is Bill,' Chitta said. 'A new client.'

'Hello, Bill,' said Tony. 'The new client.'

Bill looked up and smiled. 'Hello, Tony.'

'Sit down, Tony,' said Chitta. 'If you can take a minute from your busy pub.'

'And your dancing,' said Bill. 'If you could spare a moment from your dancing.'

JO

It was late. Moonlight was draping sheets across the square. Jo sat alone in the tiny flat above the pub, the curtain pulled back so she could see the square, but not be seen herself.

She didn't want to be seen. Not now. Not by anybody.

She'd watched them all troop out of Tony's bar in ones and twos – Laddo, Shirl, Luis, all the rest – drifting off home into the night until Tony himself had at last emerged and locked the door behind him, heading off towards his villa, leaving the square quiet and still, apart from a few die-hards who drank on in Pepe's.

And still Jo sat silent, unmoving, alone, her mind turning through the past.

There was only one photo of Jo with Clare, and Will had it. He'd taken it the week before she had died – it was a head shot, their faces close together.

They played at Jo's quite a lot. They'd rather not have done, they'd rather have been at Clare's with the piano and the central heating and as many jam butties as you could pilfer from the larder, but Laney was mardy pretty much always then and she wouldn't let them in, just shooed them off, and Nice Tony was always out at work. So they played round Jo and Will's house, bunked there across the fields. There was nobody to tell you what to do, but there was nobody to make you tea either, to look after you. There was nobody there to care.

Jo peered out into the empty square. They were beyond the anniversary of Clare's death but the past felt as close as before – darkness and feelings made an idiot of time. Jo looked across the square. She saw a figure emerge from the shadows, heading unsteadily to Pepe's. It was a figure she recognised.

Her guard was down, her heart was raw and swollen.

She was getting it wrong in Spain and what she needed now was love. She could count on one finger the times in her life she'd asked someone for help. But she was going to do that now.

Jo stood up, walked to the door.

NICK

It was happening again, the thing with the football. Nick was watching the late night highlights show with Chico. They were in Pepe's. End of the night. Nick was drunk when he came in and he was drunker now, and he had to get out.

'I'm going, Chico,' Nick said.

'Not going. Sleep with Chico.'

'Not sleep with Chico,' said Nick and stumbled from the bar.

Nick wobbled into the square. Thoughts of going were soon lost. Drink aimed Nick towards Home Sweet Home, his family's pub. There was a small flat above it, he thought, in which Jo probably now slept. And perhaps his son, though maybe Fred was staying at the villa. Nick didn't know. His thoughts were drunk-shaped, his body formless and squashy and he moved across the square like some torn bouncy castle deflating across an uneven lawn. He tottered over to the broken fountain and claimed it as base camp. He panted and groaned before aiming again for the other side of the square. Eventually he stood outside the dark, closed pub, squinting towards the single spotlight which picked out the piano on the stage.

Nick moved towards the door that led up to the flat and jabbed his key at it until he found a hole. He carefully flung the door open, gripping the handle to keep him steady and peering into a short corridor. Stairs ran up at the far end, up to the flat. Nick leapt up the stairs proudly then leapt into the room and made love to Jo like a wild baboon. He imagined he did anyway. Instead he stared up the stairs, swaying timidly before trying the door that led to the pub.

It was open. He tottered inside. Nick looked around the dark empty pub. He eyed the bottles behind the bar, visible as curved silver. Nick looked at the bar itself. A bag full of fliers hung from a hook in a corner behind it. A single bottle stood on its wooden top, next to two glasses. Nick veered over to the bar and picked up the wine. It was a good one. There was a note on a small piece of paper between the two glasses.

Miss you Nick, the note read.

Miss you too, Nick thought.

He felt sad suddenly. He had to breathe deeply to cope with the pressure of being alive. He grew jaggedly sober. He forgot about the wine and picked up the note and pocketed it and turned and walked towards the small stage. He looked at the old piano, buffed-up and centre stage but fooling nobody. He stepped carefully up onto the stage, pulled out the stool and sat down at the piano. Nick lifted the lid. There was another note inside: *Play like in Toledo.*

Nick pocketed the second note. His fingers hovered above the black and white keys. He remembered Toledo. There had been a piano in their hotel room, four flights up in some cloistered Moorish merchant's house, more ruined than charming, he'd thought back then. But Nick now recalled how the hotel glinted with romantic opulence – its peeling courtyard of fountains and vines, its smells of old wood and of rotting plaster, laughed off by sweet spritzes from the potted figs and pomegranates, from the carob and kumquat trees that guarded its geometric halls. Who knew how the piano had first arrived in their hotel room? If there had been a lift shaft to carry it, that shaft was long gone. So Jo decided the piano had been hoisted on ropes, yanked up through the courtyard then swung into place in their room.

'Why though?' Nick had asked.

'Because,' Jo invented, 'a sickly composer needed to finish his symphony.'

'Right,' Nick said. 'Of course.'

They were in a dark hotel room, shuttered up for love in the sunny afternoon. A ceiling fan chopped lazily, eddying breezes into shadowed corners. Nick was naked at the piano, hands ranging loosely across the keyboard. Jo lay on the bed, draped by a white sheet.

'And how did he get here, this sickly composer?'

'Oh, I don't know,' said Jo. 'A house guest gone wrong.'

'Right,' said Nick. 'A house guest washed up from a party.' Nick's fingers sprang jazzily across the keys. 'His playing too beautiful to ask him to leave.'

'His story too sad.'

Nick's playing slowed and turned minor.

'So let's pretend,' Jo said from the canopied bed. 'Let's pretend that you're the sickly composer.'

'Okay,' said Nick. 'Not too challenging.'

'And that I…'

'Am a nurse. And have these sex oils.'

'No, I am your muse.'

'What?'

'I am your muse.'

'If I'm ill, I don't need a bloody muse. I need a nurse.'

'With sex oils?'

'With healing hands.'

'Your malaise,' Jo vamped, 'is spiritual.'

Nick stood up and wagged his erection towards Jo. 'My malaise is not bloody spiritual.'

Jo laughed. She sat up and the sheet fell off her and she stood naked by the bed. There was a bath in the hotel room, laced with petals. She walked over and climbed in. There was a glass of white wine on a table by the bath. He watched her take a gulp, the cold wine bobbing in her warm throat as she swallowed. They were as close as they had ever been. Later that night she would tell Nick she was pregnant, that he was her family now, that she loved him now and for ever.

Nick settled at the piano and played a little, candles brightening his moving hands.

'Jo,' he said. 'In this fantasy thing, are we rich? Can we be rich?'

'*I* am very wealthy. You own nothing but your shirtsleeves and your soul.'

'Typical.'

'You have seen every quack doctor in town, taken every spa cure and treatment and medicine, and nothing can heal you.'

'Not sure I'm into that. The incurable thing.'

'Not incurable. *Medicine* can't cure you. Only music.'

'Right.'

'Only by finishing the symphony over which you have been labouring for twenty years can you be cured.'

'And tonight I finish it?'

'Yes,' Jo said.

'Then will you suck me off?'

'Play.'

Back in Toledo, Nick played freely and back in Home Sweet Home Nick opened his eyes. His fingers were fluttering above the piano keys. He was still on the stage in his parents' dark pub. Except that Jo now stood in front of him. 'Hi,' Jo said. 'You got my notes.'

She looked so bashed up, so grey, like life had turned off her drip.

'I did.' Nick patted his pocket. 'They're lovely.' He stared at her bump. 'You're...'

'Big. Yeah.' Jo placed her hands on her stomach. 'I saw you go into Pepe's. I hoped you might come here.'

'I did...'

'Where have you been?'

'In Benidorm, I..'

'What?'

'I really liked it.'

Jo laughed. 'Blair reclaims his roots.'

'I got pissed with some Vikings, but before that I went and sat and watched the old people dance again, so spic and span, twirling round, dancing in the afternoon.'

'Great.'

'So lovely to watch. So graceful. So much pain they must have felt in their lives.'

'So much love.'

'Yes. Why am I such a prick, Jo?'

'You got crumpled up early and you never got straightened out.'

'But you got more crumpled than me, Jo, and you found a way to help.'

'You could help now, Nick.' Jo looked shy. 'Can you come upstairs?'

'Why?'

She smiled. 'I'm in need of a composer.'

'Thanks,' Nick laughed. 'But I can't. I'm...'

Jo looked down at her bulge. 'Like prodding a watermelon you mean. You don't fancy me.'

'No,' Nick laughed. 'Not that. It's just...'

'You're all broken.'

'Yeah.'

'It's just a thing that you have to go through.'

'And you're waiting for me, Jo?'

'Course. For ever. Here I am.'

'And your aim is true?'

'It is. I hope it is.'

Nick watched her closely. She opened her mouth but closed it again.

'Is there something you want to tell me?' he asked.

She looked right at him, eyes locked on his. 'Maybe,' she said, then looked away.

'What does that mean?'

She didn't answer. He looked again at Jo's bump. He couldn't keep his eyes off it. His second child... His dead little sister... His fucked up mum and his fucked up dad and his fucked up, drunken life. 'You've got to go, Jo.'

'Really?'

He nodded. 'I'm no good, Jo. I'm just no good. Not yet. I've got to go.'

Jo shrugged sadly. She walked towards Nick and she bent down to the piano stool and kissed him on the cheek. She lifted up his hand and placed his palm on her stomach.

'I have two hearts beating for you, Nick.'

Jo stood. She turned around and walked slowly across the pub then disappeared through the door and off towards the stairs. She looked so slow and so old.

TONY

Tony woke into darkness with a terrified start.

Where was he? What was this place? This wasn't right.

His breath calmed; his head cleared. Oh yes. He was in *his room*, the room they used to call the spare room before he moved out of the bedroom he shared with Laney.

His hand dabbed round an unfamiliar bedside table until he found the switch. He clicked the bedside light on. He blinked, checked the time. Nearly three a bloody clock in the morning. He felt raw and alone.

Tony sat up in bed and put his feet down onto the little rug. His feet hunted around for their slippers. He wanted to go in to her. He looked up to his dressing gown, hanging on the door hook like a resting ghost. Tony looked over to the small bedside table. Now that he was in the spare room there were *two* photos next to his bed.

When he'd been in with Laney he'd only had one, a photo of their wedding day, taken outside the church in the village. That photo was in a simple silver frame. He picked it up. Laney and Tony were holding hands and stepping from the church porch after the ceremony. The family stood around them, throwing rice and confetti. Laney had her veil up and was dimpled and smiling, ready for life. Tony was proud but grim. He was looking off, away from the camera. Laney always said he was looking to the chipper over the road, wondering about his stomach.

In the photo, Laney's parents were stood behind her shoulder, with the bearing of crumpled ancients, but only really about forty.

At forty, people these days were just getting round to thinking what to do with themselves, whereas by then Laney's folks were already eyeing up their coffins.

Tony's parents were behind his shoulder too. But they weren't stood there. They were buried there, beneath the churchyard's massive yew. They'd died two years before, within three months of each other. Tony had been nineteen. He'd thought about them on his wedding day; he wished they'd been alive. But given they weren't he'd been glad they were at least close by.

In the spare room, Tony looked at the wedding photo. He looked at the yew tree with the two family graves beneath. There were three family graves there these days. Tony put down the wedding photo and picked up the second photo, the one only fit for the spare room. It was a photo of Clare, his little girl, standing in the back garden, wearing her favourite dress.

There was a sound outside his room. He startled, sat still. The noise came again.

The hallway light clicked on. The door opened. It was Laney. She looked pale. She had her favourite nightie on. Her shins were lathered in eczema cream.

'I saw your light on,' she said. 'I can't sleep.'

'Oh right,' said Tony. 'Not like you. You had your pills?'

She nodded. 'Have you?'

Tony nodded too. 'It's not your thingy is it?'

'No, it's not that. Did you do the garage?'

He nodded. 'And the pool.'

'I did the back door.'

'I know. I checked.'

'Right.'

'Right then.'

Silence intruded.

'Will you come in, Tony? Sleep in our bed.'

His heart was twanging like a country guitar. Happiness sprang across him like a dusting of sugar. After all these years of being with her, a hint that she wanted him and all his resolutions seemed to melt in the air. They tried to melt at least. But he'd not fall back into old ways just yet. He had a bit of strength yet. 'Thanks,' Tony said simply. 'But I can't.'

'Oh,' Laney said. She looked surprised.

'You can come in here though,' said Tony, all cheerful. He flipped the blanket on his single bed further back to show willing. 'Have a snuggle.'

Laney stared at the single bed. She seemed to relax and she took a step forwards. Then she spotted something and stopped – the photo of Clare by his bed.

'You're okay,' Laney said sharply, backing off. 'I'll make a tea. Try and get off in my own bed.'

'Oh,' it was Tony's turn now to say.

He wanted to hold her. This wasn't them, this distance and uncertainty, these glum, far-away figures. They were Tony and Laney, the dream team, the old firm, one for two and two for one, they couldn't be kept apart. Apart from now.

'Right then,' said Laney.

'Right.'

'Night then,' said Laney.

'Night then love. I mean Laney.'

'Night, Tony.'

She stepped back out of his room, closing the door behind her.

It was morning, hot and clear.

Tony peered in through the window at Pam and Keith's, into their sun lounge at the back of the villa. The place was empty, the furniture all gone, their villa still not sold.

But he wasn't going to get caught, Tony. He was going to flog his bloody pub if it was the last thing he did. That'd get him home. He was going to give this up too, next month, this pool cleaning. The pub needed every minute he could give, especially now this Bill had shown his hand. He'd asked if he could scrutinise Tony's books. He'd mentioned the idea of also taking their villa in a package. Just hold a good line and Tony would soon be back in Yorkshire, scoffing a growler with onion chutney in some friendly little café on the Moors.

But would he be there on his own?

His feelings jagged around. Tony had no idea what he was doing. But then again he'd never been so sure. He texted Jo again but again there was no reply.

He put his rucksack down and walked over to the pool house to get the brush and the chemicals. The door was ajar, not locked, and Tony leant in. He didn't even look in the corners anymore for his little friend the bird.

The bird had realised that the door wasn't locked, and now Tony had realised too. He took the pool brush, screwed the longest handle to the end of it and dipped it into the pool, pushing it right down to the bottom. Tony gave the brush a shove along the pool floor and watched a film of silt spring off the tiles. He felt good, Tony, he felt strong. He shoved the brush again.

Tony heard a sound, a sort of reedy piping. He heard it again. Then a little scuffling sound. He looked round, saw it straight away, perched on the pool house roof. It was a tiny thing, titchy. Tony wasn't good with birds and he couldn't tell if this one was his old mate or not.

But it just sat there on the roof looking over at him.

The sun streamed in through the window of the small bedroom. Tony stared at the photo of Clare then placed it back next to his bed. He stepped out of the bedroom and stepped across the hall. Tony quietly opened the door into the big bedroom, the room he used to share with Laney.

Fred was in there, sleeping on a kid's bed, his white feet splayed out of the bottom of a white sheet. Tony pulled the door carefully closed. He moved down the hall, peered into the lounge. Laney was in there, watching TV with a brew.

Tony turned and looked at himself in the hallway mirror. He was wearing the shirt Laney had bought him for his birthday, the one he didn't like. People liked to see the presents they'd given and Tony had put it on to be nice, to show her that even if it was rough between them he wasn't being an arse about things. He'd worn the shirt for that, yes, but also to try and butter her up, to try and soften the blow. Because he had something difficult to say, Tony, something that kept catching in his mouth, finding a reason not to emerge.

'Come on, Tony mate,' he whispered to himself. He took a little breath then made an entrance, arms held aloft, doing a little twirl. 'What do you reckon?'

Laney looked over. 'Oh,' she dead-panned. 'Reckon you'll knock 'em dead.'

'First time I've worn it.'

'Apart from your birthday.'

'Hardly then. Laddo spilled on it.'

'I remember.'

'You bought it for me.'

'I know which blumming shirt it is. Why you wearing it?'

'What do you think? Captain bloody Marvel, eh?'

'Come here,' Laney said.

Tony smiled. Even though they were barely speaking she couldn't resist straightening him up. She stood and stepped over. He was going to tell her the news. He opened his mouth but nothing came out. He watched her as her eyes scanned his shirt.

'Still got a stain on it,' she said.

'Give over Laney, it hasn't.'

'It has. There.' She pointed to his neck.

'It doesn't matter.'

'It does matter.'

'You can barely see it.'

'But you can see it, Tony.'

'*You* can.'

'You can't go out like that.'

Tony felt hopeless, like there was nothing he could say or do, like there were no rights but wrongs with Laney now. Everywhere he trod he found eggshells.

'Bollocks,' he said. 'I only wore it to be nice.'

'What?' said Laney. 'What have I done?'

'You're always picking holes.'

'You are, you mean.'

'Bloody holes in everything.'

Accusation and counter-accusation; every word a deeper hole.

He couldn't tell her now.

He had been going to tell Laney that Bill was coming in to Home Sweet Home, that a deal would likely be reached; that he'd need her signature on documents, her ideas on what she wanted when they'd sold up the nest. But how could he talk to her about hard things – he looked down at his garish cuffs – when they couldn't even talk about a crappy bloody shirt?

Tony had watched most of his friends divorce then remarry, turn around and do the whole dance again, while he and Laney dwelt on the side lines, banking time until suddenly they had fifty years.

Almost fifty years. And guess what?

Maybe that was long enough. Maybe him and Laney were the odd ones, the closets that had played it wrong, standing there with their statins and their biopsies and their five-a-bloody-day, eyeing up a sixth straight decade of marriage, having just found out lately what all others had long known, that love can't stop a life from fraying.

Wear and tear was all they had now; the darn they'd used to fix their love was thicker than the love itself. Tony opened his mouth to speak, but Laney got there first. 'You can't go out in a dirty shirt. They'll think that nobody loves you.'

Something just clicked in his head. 'They'd be right.'

'What?'

'Nobody does love me.'

'You what?'

'You don't. Not anymore.'

'Give over.'

'You're so cold. Always angry, always pretending you're not angry.'

'You been speaking to Jo?'

'Why don't you say what's on your mind, Laney?'

'What?'

'Say it, Laney. Admit the worst thing, the thing you're most afraid to say.'

'What?'

'The stone you lug about for a heart.'

'Tony!'

'Say it.'

'What?'

He paused. 'That I should have kept an eye out.'

Laney looked away.

'That I should have been more careful.'

Laney clenched her hands into fists.

'That if you'd have been there it wouldn't have happened.'

She tilted her head back, flared her nostrils. 'It wouldn't have happened, Tony.'

'Right.'

'It was on your watch.'

It *had* been on Tony's watch. Laney had popped out for half an hour. Nick was upstairs in his room. Clare was playing on her own in the garden. Tony was at home in the kitchen peeling spuds.

'It *was* on your bloody watch, Tony.'

'I know, Laney.'

'You can't say it wasn't on your watch.'

'Say you blame me. Admit it.'

She looked him dead in the eye. 'I blame you.'

He'd long known it, felt the thousand icy darts of Laney's blame pricking away at him, every cold look from her eyes, every put-down in her voice, he'd known what it meant. She'd never blabbed it, but every single action chattered at the truth.

His head flopped forward, his stomach pitched and heaved. Tony turned and bolted out of the house.

'Tony!' she called after him, but he was gone.

The gravel on the path seemed to crunch in his ears, breath grated at his chest. Time battered chimes from the church bell. He was going to leave her. He was going to pack her in.

Blaming him? As if he'd not thought the same thing himself a thousand times a day.

Blaming him? His blood was like lava, his breath like a roar.

He marched towards the village, spotted its dome ahead.

What was that she'd said, the night of his last birthday?

It's better than the brochure.

Bollocks it was. He panted, reached for his breath. Goat bells clanged on the mountain, but Tony didn't hear them. A donkey brayed close in the groves. He marched along the track, huffing and puffing. He'd show Laney. Bill would be there tonight and Tony would flog the bloody pub. He was jiggered if he'd hop meekly in the hearse.

The past was done – *her blaming him?* – but the future was waiting tonight.

Tony made the village. He marched beyond the *bodega*, up by the shuttered houses and up past the half-finished flats, a stripe of dusk sky following him unseen above the high narrow streets. The widow who ran the tobacconist was sat in the road in a deck chair. Music climbed out from her open front door.

'*Jos hermano*,' she called to Tony, raising her glass.

Tony didn't hear her, just marched right on.

'*Jos*,' the baker's girl called to his back.

Voices grew louder as he made the square – the white-washed church, the dry stone fountain. Tony looked towards Pepe's. It was heaving, people spilling out of the doorway and out onto the square. His heart sank. He looked across to Home Sweet Home. That was heaving too.

All the tables they'd slung out onto the square had been taken and all the way inside, right up to the bar, people stood and drank, or else ate at the tables or danced by the stage. It'd never been so full. At least he'd never seen it. Bill would have to be impressed with this.

Tony walked across the square, spotting faces. There was Claes and Marja, sharing a funny fag on the pavement with the lad Raul who worked at the garage on the coast road.

'Yeah! Tony!' Marja shouted.

'Amigo,' said Raul.

Tony nodded quickly at Raul. He suffered Marja's cuddle, his eyes scanning quickly over her shoulder for Bill.

'Nice shirt!' said Claes. 'Your party shirt!'

'It's my birthday shirt. I put it on for...'

'Happy birthday, Tony,' shouted Marja, kissing him.

'It's not my...'

'Hey, happy birthday, man,' Raul said to Tony, shaking his hand.

'*Happy birthday to you,*' they started singing to Tony.

'Thanks, it's not my... I was making a...' Tony said, passing inside.

There was a mob in front of the bar so as he could barely see the thing, but he could see above it through to the empty hook in the corner that they'd hung the flier bag on.

The bar was heaving. Jo was still away, not answering her phone or the flat door, so the bar had a couple more kids from the village helping serve, lads this time, the trombonist and sax player. They were pouring drinks. Handing over glasses, taking cash, giving change. Every table was full. People twirled to the music that Shirl and the trumpeters played. Font and Penny were dancing together. Font had some tapas in his moustache. Laddo was dancing with Consuela with the huge hennaed hair. Laddo was pissed and happy and full of clumsy gusto. The sweat from his nose was beading up nicely onto his big glasses.

'Shirt!' Laddo shouted to Tony when he saw him. 'Shirt! Shirt! Shirt!'

'It's Tony's birthday,' shouted Marja, coming inside. '*Happy birthday to you.*'

'It's not my birthday.' Tony appealed. 'Tell them, Laddo.'

But Laddo just laughed. '*Happy birthday,*' he sang, twirling Consuela round.

The sleepy mayor was now tugging at Tony's elbow, offering congratulations.

'It's not my...'

'*Happy birthday, dear Tony,*' Gabriel sang quietly.

'Thanks, Gabriel.'

Bugger this, thought Tony. He was hot and bothered. It was all too much. Tony looked around madly for Bill. And there he was, clutching his brown briefcase. Number one client. Tony's saviour. Laney blaming him. He'd sell the bloody pub.

Bill was standing by the dance floor with Pepe and Lita. Tony marched over.

'Here again,' Tony teased Pepe. 'Can't keep away.'

'Tonight we are celebrating,' said Lita. 'Pepe, I want to dance.'

'Excuse us,' said Pepe, as Lita led him into the crowd of dancers. Tony eyed his buyer nervously.

'Happy birthday,' said Bill, looking up at Tony.

'It's not my birthday.'

'Happy birthday anyway. For when it is. In case I miss it.'

'Thanks. Same to you.'

'Thanks. I'm Taurus. Bill the Bull. Do you believe in horoscopes, Tony?' asked Bill.

Laddo twirled past, held by Consuela. 'Did you get the stains out?' said Laddo.

'What?' said Bill.

'He means from my shirt,' Tony explained. 'No I don't,' he said.

'Don't what?' said Bill.

'Don't believe in horoscopes.'

'Nor do I,' said Bill. 'As a rule. Although this morning's was a bit...'

'It looks splodgy,' said Laddo, twirling round again.

'That's the pattern,' said Tony. 'Bugger off.'

'Oh right,' said Laddo's red spinning face. 'Splodgy pattern.'

Tony had to get away. It was boiling. Too noisy to talk to Bill.

'Get some air?' Tony gasped. 'Find a quiet place to talk?'

'There's one on the collar,' Laddo pointed, spinning past again.

'One what?' said Bill.

'He means a stain.'

'Oh right. I have had acupuncture though,' Bill told Tony. 'And the wife had her palm read.'

'The one with the needles,' said Tony.

'No, they just looked at her hand.'

'I meant the acupuncture,' said Tony.

'Course,' said Bill. 'I was joking.'

'I can see something on the collar,' said Laddo. 'That's not a splodge.'

'Piss off, Laddo.'

'Dirty shirt,' said Laddo. 'Wouldn't be seen dead in it.'

Tony didn't even reply. The piano played. The trumpets parped. He looked at Bill. Why couldn't they just do it? He just wanted to shake on a price. Tony's head was killing. He was sweating like a horse. Blaming him. People sang *Happy Birthday*, though most no longer knew to who. Why couldn't Bill just get down to it?

'About your pub...' Bill said, holding on to his brown briefcase and looking up at Tony. 'I'm not buying it.'

'What?'

'I'm buying Pepe's.'

'What?'

'He's giving it to me for a knock-down price.'

There was an awful noise, a terrible screaming.

'Just business,' said Bill, but Tony was now looking over his head. 'Nothing personal.'

Tony looked to the little wooden dance floor. He saw some big glasses broken on the floor. He saw his mate Laddo had fallen and was clutching his chest, a panicked space opening around him, Consuela screaming. Shirl jumped up from the piano and Tony was over too, and Laddo's face was locked and red and his eyes were wild and scared and staring.

LANEY

Laney sat in the spare room at the villa, perched on the single bed. Tears ran down her face. She was holding the photo of Clare that Tony kept by his bed, but she was off with the memories in her head.

It was high summer, windows open. The piano stool was long enough for them both to perch and Nick was working the peddles as they plonked away at the keys.

'*Row, row, row,*' sang little Clare, and Nick joined in.

'No, silly pants,' Clare said. 'I sing the first line *then* you do.'

Laney watched from the hallway.

'*Row row row your boat,*' sang Clare.

'*Gently down the stream,*' sang Clare, as Nick sang, '*Row row row your boat.*'

'*Merrily, merrily, merrily, merrily,*' sang Clare, with Nick following her a line behind.

'*Life is but a dream.*'

A breeze puffed up the curtains. Sunshine painted the wall. They carried on singing, round and round and round.

UNLESS...

TONY

Tony met Shirl as she came out of the door.

She still held the pen from signing the forms, though she didn't know that she had it. Her face was caved in and her eyes weren't looking outwards. Gently, like leading an animal, Tony guided Shirl down corridors as doctors and nurses moved by under white lights. Double doors slipped open and they stepped out into the warm dark.

He shepherded Shirl across the road into the car park, towards his passenger door. But she passed that door and stood by the back door so he opened that and helped her in that way instead. *You can climb in through the bloody window if you want*, thought Tony. *You can do what you like today.*

Tony got in the driver's seat and settled. He looked at Shirl in the rear-view. It was dark in the back but Tony could see Shirl looking sideways out of the window. She looked smaller and older than anyone he'd ever seen. Tony slid the key into the ignition but did not start the car.

What did Shirl want? Should he start the engine and take her home? Tony sat back into the driver's seat and waited. Every time she breathed he could feel her pain moving about in the car.

'I'd better text my son Martin,' eventually she said.

'Another few hours won't hurt.'

'He'll want to make his arrangements.'

'He can make his arrangements in the morning when he's had his kip. His kids are young, you know. He's bound to need his kip.'

'Suppose you're right. What about Laddo's manky sister?'

'Oh, bollocks to that bag-hound,' said Tony. 'She'll only want to hear the will.'

Shirl laughed. 'She speaks very highly of you.'

The car went quiet.

'Have you told your Laney yet?'

'No.' Tony eyed Shirl in the rear-view. 'What do you want to do?'

'Curl up,' eventually she said, 'and die.'

Tony sat alone in the car outside Shirl's villa. His car lights were off, but inside the villa lights blazed and shone their rectangles across the dark garden. It took an hour or more, but Tony watched the lounge then the kitchen lights click off, then the bathroom light come on then off, then all that was left was a small bedside light which glowed around the side of the dark bedroom blinds.

She'd have a long night, Shirl.

Tony started the car. He drove towards his own villa. It wasn't far. He stopped the engine just before he got there. Not because he was worried about waking Fred. You could swing that lad round by his heels and he'd never wake up once he was gone. No, it was Laney he was wary of. Waking her. Talking to her. The things that had been said. The things he'd have to say.

He couldn't face that.

Tony climbed out of the dark car and walked towards the driveway that ran down the side of his villa. He headed towards the garage at the drive's end then walked round the back of the garage into the back garden. The chairs were out on the patio beside the pool, just like they were the night of his birthday. Tony walked round the top of the pool. He knelt down by Laney's favourite sunlounger. It was the comfiest one they could find. Fold-up. Hardly cheap.

Tony folded the lounger and carried it back round the top of the pool, across the patio and down to the front of the house. He popped his car boot open and slid the lounger inside.

Tony shut the boot and climbed inside.

*

He got inside Home Sweet Home and locked the front door behind him.

He wanted to speak to not one bugger.

Jo and Luis had a key to the front door, so Tony bolted that from the inside. He locked the back door by the kitchen, which only he had the key for, then he locked and bolted the door from the hallway that led to the upstairs flat. Right, no bastard was getting in now.

Tony put the sunlounger down then unfolded it into a bed.

He sat down on it, heavy and tired, and looked around the pub. He was right in the middle of the room. It felt exposed. Tony stood and carried the sunlounger across the pub and slid it snugly in behind the bar. Tony went round and sat down on the sunlounger.

Better. He was hidden better now.

Tony lay down behind the bar. He looked up at the bottles of booze upside down in the optics above him, glass glinting in the darkness. He'd have a bit of that. He sat up, reached over for a glass, stretched up to the optic, clicked himself a double, which he necked before pouring another. He necked that too and took another. Tony put his arm up behind his head and used the crook of it as a pillow, like he'd done as a kid when he'd been camping, or just laying on the grass looking up. Oh, he'd fucked it all up now.

Bang, went a sound on the pub's front window.

Tony sat bolt up and peered across the bar.

Bang bang, it sounded again as the whole glass wobbled.

He looked through the glass of Home Sweet Home and out onto the dark pavement. What was that? A small figure banging a knuckle on the window. In their other hand the figure was holding a stick. 'I've got a gun,' they shouted. 'Whoever you are.'

'Jo you daft cow,' Tony said, standing and walking towards the door. 'That twig loaded?'

'I thought you were a...'

'I'm not,' Tony said, looking at her through the glass. He downed his double.

'I thought you'd have called me from the hospital.'

Tony said nothing.

'Does Laney know about Laddo?' asked Jo.

'No,' said Tony.

'Nor does Nick,' said Jo. 'Just us two.'

'Me and thee,' Tony said. 'The odd couple.'

'Open up,' she said.

Tony looked through the dark window to Jo on the other side. He was going to have to tell her. 'Since you've come to the valley,' Tony started, 'you've understood me and you've helped me stand up for myself.'

'Can we do this speech with a cup of coffee, Tony?'

The dark words were lining up inside his throat, little bullets in a gun. 'But since you've come out here pretending to be on holiday without telling anyone you were preggers, since you've come out here to meddle with my family, I've ended up kipping in the spare room for the first time in my married life, my son's waltzed off in Benidorm, never to be seen again, and my best mate's died disco dancing.'

'Tony...'

'And I'm not even done there, am I Jo? Because thanks to you wheedling and conniving and sheep-dogging everybody behind everybody else's backs, getting half the valley keyed up to change their bloody lives, the ghost of our Clare is out walking again and my wife is blaming me.'

'For what?'

'What *might* she be blaming me for?'

Jo flinched. 'That wasn't your fault.'

Tony fixed her with a hard eye. 'Sure of that, are you?'

Jo looked at the pavement.

'You've stirred everything up, Jo.'

'But...'

'It's not what I wanted.'

Jo was staring at Tony, her face growing pale.

'So thank you very much,' Tony said, each word a hard little punch, 'for standing there defending the pub with a stick, and thank you for wanting to have a brew with me, and for all other services rendered to the Metcalfe family, but I don't want your help anymore, and I'm done with sticking up for myself, and I'm done with babying Laney, and I'm done with getting home and I should have just kept my bloody trap shut and stayed in the shit like everyone else.'

He backed off from the window into the gloom.

'I'm done,' he said and turned his back on her. 'I'm done with the bollocking lot of it.'

JO

Done?

Tony was done with it?

Perfect. Fine. Excellent. Because she was done too.

She watched Tony walk away, shade into the blackness at the back of the pub until all she could make out was the blacker shape of the bar behind which he stepped.

The piano stood alone on the stage and Jo stood alone on the pavement.

She listened.

First there was silence, then came the sound of a bottle clinking against glass, then footsteps padding into the dark kitchen and drawers being rifled through. Then the pad of footsteps came again, this time back towards the bar, followed by a faint sound of flaring.

A match-head burst into flame, lighting the cigarette which Jo quickly glimpsed in Tony's illuminated mouth. He was leaning on the bar, elbows next to a bottle of scotch. Tony shook the flame out, zigzagging light across the bar.

'What you smoking for?'

Tony didn't reply. The glow of the cigarette tip moved down behind the bar. No sound in the village. No sound from the bar.

'Is that it then,' said Jo, 'the end of our buddy movie?'

Silence.

'It was a dull film anyway.'

Nothing.

'Who wants to see a story about a clapped-out expat, moulding away in a fly-blown town? Who cares if he changes or not, rises to the challenges of his shitty life? So what if he does? It's not exactly sexy, is it, Tony Tone Tone? You're a skint old duffer in a shit old town.'

She stopped. There was nothing but the sound of her own ragged breath. But now she was angry at herself for having cursed him. 'And as for me. What kind of buddy sidekick am I? I don't make things better. I just screw things up.'

Jo had thought you could get over things. She had thought you could get over problems if you held yourself properly, allowed pain to flow through you like a river, not dam it up inside you and drown. And it had worked. She *had* overcome things. The shit-house parents she'd been born to. She'd got over them. She could have gone under. Many times she did. Calamity clawed inside her. But she had let pain flow through her like a river, and she had overcome.

But not everything.

Jo hadn't overcome everything.

There was one dam still, deep inside her.

She could just say it now, hand the shitty stick on to Tony, let that old bastard deal with it. What would he make of it?

Three poisonous words.

They were easy enough to say. Hardly bloody Mandarin.

She looked into the dark of the silent bar. The words in her mouth like three bombs in the hold. But something held her back. The wag of the orange light as he held the cigarette to his mouth maybe? Simple stubbornness? She didn't know. But something clicked in her head. She couldn't let the old dick down just yet.

She would tell him what she had learned about life and change, what the thing she'd done had taught her. 'This is known as the hard bit,' Jo told Tony. 'And it's known as the hard bit because it's the hard bit.'

She paused.

Nothing.

'What you are feeling now, Tony, is the shit being burned off, the ghost's last hold on your throat... Real change is hard.'

Jo listened, heard a glass being drained then refilled. Another match was struck.

'You can feel pain,' said Jo. 'And turn it into something better.'

Did she believe that? She didn't know. But she knew they were in for a long one. He was a stubborn old sod normally, but now he was mad with it too. It was like a hostage situation, with her as the negotiator, except Tony had kidnapped himself.

She looked around the dark square. Things felt miles wrong. Her stomach fell then twisted. Laddo was dead, Nick was gone, Tony was wired tighter than she'd thought.

And if Laney was blaming Tony, well, the state he was in, it wouldn't take long until he took that on. Because that was people when they opened up to change – angled a knife at the crack in their shell – they became susceptible, liable to self-harm, prone to lighting fires.

There was no telling what he might do.

'Can we skip the dark night and go straight to morning?' But she already knew the answer to that.

She looked again into the silent bar, saw the orange tip of the cigarette arc up towards where his mouth must have been. She knew he was looking right at her, even if he wouldn't speak. Fine. She'd wait it out.

'Hey, Tony you loony,' she said, pointing up at the flat. 'I'll be up there waiting.'

No reply.

Jo walked towards the door at the side of Home Sweet Home and took the stairs to the flat. She stepped inside. The cot was empty; the bed was empty too. She stepped over and opened the balcony door. She lifted the chair and placed it by the open door. She sat down and looked out across the square, then she texted Nick to tell him about Laddo.

Jo sat all night, keeping watch – tired and pregnant, ragged, haunted – and through the night the weight never left her, the weight of the three little bombs in her throat.

TONY

He woke squinting. If eyes can grimace then Tony's did.

Everywhere was parched and bright. Tony was thirsty but he didn't have the spit to swallow. His skull was a timpani smashing down a mountain. He reached for a drink, swigged at some wine, made an awful noise.

He coughed then drank then he made the noise again. He drank again and coughed. He put the bottle down. His hands grabbed at the sides of the sunlounger and he looked across the pub. He twigged where he was. The windows were a long glaze of sunlight, the square behind like some theatre set he was dreaming. He swung his legs out, put his feet on the floor. Tony still had his shoes on. He still had his birthday shirt on.

Tony heard footsteps from the flat above.

He peered across the pub. There was an ashtray and some fags on the bar. Where did they come from? He looked at the ashtray. God. He'd smoked a couple too. Tony picked up a bottle and came round the bar and walked towards the windows and looked across the square. Sunshine shoved its thumbs into his eyes. He squinted across the square, past the broken fountain over towards Pepe's.

Who was that?

Tony made a visor of his hand to shade his eyes. He looked again. Bill was stood outside Pepe's. He had his brown briefcase. Chitta, Tony's accountant, was stood next to Bill. They were smartly dressed and Chitta checked her watch. The church clock chimed. A car came into the square and stopped. Tony knew the car.

Pepe got out and then Lita got out too.

They walked over to Chitta and Bill. Pepe hugged Chitta, his cousin, then he shook Bill's hand. Lita did the same, and they went inside Pepe's.

The four took a table by the window. Tony was standing in the shade, so they did not see him, but it was easy for Tony to see as Chitta pulled out papers for Bill and Pepe to sign.

Tony watched as Bill bought Pepe's.

Tony had a drink. He dragged the sunlounger further behind the bar and lay down. It was the darkest place he could find. But it wasn't dark enough. It was not dark enough to hide from shame. He was ashamed of himself for believing in things – that life might be different.

He should have kept his peace and toddled along, not charged back into life asking it for more, asking it for too much, stirring all these wasps up in all these bloody nests.

There's no bugger dafter than a daft old bugger.

Tony felt duped and stupid. He had another drink.

His head was gone and he felt about a hundred.

The worst of it all was what Laney said was true.

Fred was stood there suddenly, alone in a patch of sunlight on the pavement outside Home Sweet Home. 'Bastard!' Fred shouted.

If Tony twisted his neck on the sunlounger he could peer down the side of the bar and see the lad. He could see nobody with Fred, though presumably Laney, or some other carer, must have been standing nearby.

'Bastard!' Fred said again. 'Granddad breakdown!' he added.

Tony had a drink. Fixed him with a salty eye.

'Total breakdown!' Fred shouted. 'Total mental breakdown!'

It went on all day. It was like Tony was in a cage, like he was some animal that everyone could wander over to and upset whenever they fancied, waggle a stick at him, laugh at his plight. He'd definitely chosen the wrong place to hide. Middle of the village with a great big window in front of him. What a closet. He had another drink.

Tony thought about bolting out the front and hopping into his car and driving off. He thought about that quite a lot, was perhaps about to do it once, but then he saw Consuela walk across the square towards him, looking like it was her turn to rattle his cage. And rattle she did. She pulled at the door, tugged at it, trying to get in for her coffee. She was vexed he wasn't open. She looked rattled herself, upset and frail. Laddo had died in her arms, more or less. She stood on the pavement and made a call then she walked slowly off. Tony had a drink.

Luis came next, nosing to a stop on his moped, inches from the glass. He climbed off and took off his helmet to reveal his bandana. He stepped forward. Luis pressed his nose onto the bolted glass door. He made a visor of a cupped hand and touched that hand onto the glass, peering underneath it into the dark pub.

'Tony? Tony?' Luis called, eyes darting around inside. 'I want to work.'

Luis waited. 'Tony,' he said. 'Tony. Open up.'

He paced up and down outside the windows a few times.

'You are not the only one, Tony,' he said. 'You are not the only one.'

Luis got on his moped and pulled on his helmet and left. Tony had a drink.

Then it was Font's turn for a cameo on Tony's little stage.

From where he lay behind the bar, Tony heard footsteps and a rattle on the bolted front door and then Font say, 'Bloody closed.'

Tony watched Font reel away from the door.

'Closed!' Font shouted, his world collapsing like a toddler's. But unlike a toddler, Font's mobile was out and he made a call.

'Closed, Pen,' he said. 'I know, Pen. We're booked in for brunch. That tit Tony.'

That tit Tony listened and watched. He had a drink.

'Wasn't expecting Claes and Marja to come back last night, Pen. But I'm glad they did.' Font did a purring sound into the phone. 'You were sensational.'

Tony icked a bit and rolled away. He'd stopped watching but he couldn't help listening. 'I'll grab some food to cook at ours,' said Font. 'For four.'

Font went and Rosa and Maria came next. They had their instrument cases with them. They were both on to work lunch then play music afterwards. It seemed that a death in the pub hadn't changed their plans.

'Tony,' they shouted.

They knew he was in there. Word gets around. As shown when Consuela came back later and asked Tony to come out. And when Font came back too and said, 'Eavesdropping, Tony, is very bad manners,' and then went.

But for the moment it was Rosa and Maria standing there.

'We want to work,' Maria said.

'We want to play,' Rosa said.

They put their cases down on the pavement and took out their trumpets and honked towards the pub as some kind of protest and then they left.

The villagers wouldn't leave him alone. And he wouldn't leave the bottle alone. He was still in his shirt. It was getting on dusk. He'd had nothing to eat all day. The floorboards creaked in the flat above.

Next to take the stage was Pepe. He put on a right performance. Best yet, all things told. The first Tony knew of Pepe's arrival was when he heard a clatter from the square and moved his head to see what it was. From inside his shadow behind the bar, Tony saw Pepe out in the square, stood between the water fountain and Home Sweet Home.

By Pepe's feet was a big wooden box. Pepe held a fold-out stool in one hand, which he put down, and he had an easel tied with string across his back, which he slipped out of then folded out so that it stood facing Home Sweet Home. Tony watched Pepe disappear inside Pepe's, returning quickly with a canvas which he placed on the easel.

Sitting down on the now-unfolded stool, Pepe opened the wooden box and took out a palette, some brushes, paints. Tony looked at Pepe in the square, the white shine of Venus above the white-washed church growing brighter as dusk settled across the village. Tony watched Pepe paint.

Last time Tony had seen Pepe paint they had been in the olive groves, weeks ago, before Nick and Jo and Fred came, before Tony had made a go of the pub and fallen out with Laney, before Laddo had died and Pepe had betrayed him.

Pepe *had* betrayed Tony, hadn't he?

What was that Pepe had said when they were out in the groves and Pepe was painting something totally different, seeing something in his mind that wasn't even there. What was it? Tony rummaged around, he knew he'd have it somewhere, he chose to remember it at the time. Yes, there it was, 'I have another life waiting somewhere,' he had said.

And for a while Tony had felt like that, that there was another life out there, or almost there – a future waiting for him to step into, a version of Tony who was flogging the bar and the villa and stepping on a plane back to Blighty, a bolstered, happy Tony questing off home. But Tony didn't feel like that anymore. He didn't feel like he was embarking on some new version of himself; he felt all the old versions grabbing at him and sucking him backwards into despair. He felt one version in particular claw at him. The version who had been on watch. Tony was down there inside himself, eyeing up his own worst place, the part of himself he had buried and hidden, the part of himself of which he was most ashamed.

Had he blamed himself without knowing for all those years? Was it that he had been so meek and amiable, so eager to bloody please? Tony had another drink. He looked over to Pepe. The bastard.

Tony leapt to his feet, swerved round from behind the bar and ran towards the door which he unlocked and unbolted in two known movements and then he flung the door open and belted across the square towards Pepe, who looked surprised as Tony neared and then – boot – Tony kicked at the legs of the small painting stool that

Pepe was sitting on and the legs skidded and Pepe's legs flew up and he fell sideways off the stool and landed on his arse in the square, his brush still in his hand, looking up at Tony with more composure in his eyes than he ought to have had. 'What are you doing, Tony?'

'What are you doing, Pepe?'

'Painting you a picture.'

Tony looked at the canvas. 'What is it?'

'Your pub.'

'That's not my pub. Doesn't look like my pub.'

'It does to me. Are you going to help?' Pepe stuck out his hand. It had a splodge of red paint on it. Tony looked at Pepe's hand then turned and walked back towards Home Sweet Home.

'Tony,' he heard Pepe call after him. 'Bill was never interested. He pretended so he could see your books. *To get the edge on you*, I think you English call it. I did not know.'

The words hit Tony and he blushed in his chest. He'd been more of a fool than he'd thought. There hadn't even been a chance of a sale.

'Right then,' said Tony stupidly. 'Right bloody then.'

He backed off, scared and drunk, back across the square. Tony made his pub, grabbed the door, yanked it closed behind him, locked and bolted it. He'd been an ape, a total cretin. He went back behind the bar, hating himself and hating his pub and hating every footstep that he took. He guzzled some whisky and he guzzled some wine. The sicker it made him the better that was.

'Right then,' said Tony.

Then his legs went, and he lay down unsteady, lop-sided and mad on the sunlounger and he guessed he must have slept because then he heard little Clare's voice telling him that Nick had to do it, that Nick had to play, and then, 'Tony! Tony!' was the next thing he heard.

He moved his head, looked towards the door.

It was dark outside, but there was someone there. A figure.

She was sitting on a plastic chair on the pavement, with her white linen shawl turbaned round her head. She was sitting right next to the door, looking into the dark pub. She had wine and an old newspaper tucked under her arm. She tossed the newspaper down on the pavement in front of her. 'Come here, Tony,' she said, 'And sit with me.'

Tony shifted on the sunlounger in the dark.

'That my sunlounger creaking, Tony Metcalfe? That's my favourite one you've pilfered.'

Silence.

'Somebody told me,' Laney said between drinks of the wine she held. 'About a man named Bill who carries a little brown briefcase.'

Here we go, thought Tony. He heard the booze in her voice.

'Finished,' said Laney, draining her glass. 'But you've got a whole bloody bar in there.'

Tony looked up to the optics shining in the dark.

'Now this man Bill, he wanted to buy a pub.'

Tony sat up. Matches rattled in his pocket. He climbed off the sunlounger and picked up a bottle of red and an opener and glass and he walked towards the door. Tony walked over near to where Laney sat and he looked at her through the dark glass of the locked front door.

'You're some state,' she said, eyeing him. 'You've ruined that shirt.'

He said nothing.

'Oh,' she said. 'I brought you this.'

Laney picked the folded old newspaper up from the pavement and she shoved it through the letterbox of Home Sweet Home. It landed inside on the floor and flapped half open. Tony looked down and saw it was the paper Laddo had given Tony on his birthday, the copy of the *Yorkshire Evening Post* that they'd found in a Benidorm bar.

'Something to read,' said Laney, 'Must be a bit dull in there for you.'

Tony stared at the paper.

'Some news from home,' Laney said.

Tony put the wine and the glass and the corkscrew on the pub floor and turned round. He lifted a chair, placed it so that it was about a foot from Laney's own chair out on the pavement. He sat down and picked up the corkscrew and the bottle and started opening the wine.

'Now this man named Bill,' said Laney, 'who wanted a pub. He knew a man named Tony.'

'And this Tony,' Tony said, 'had a pub to sell.'

'Not to sell, no,' spat Laney. 'Having got no consent.'

Tony tapped the neck of the open wine bottle against the glass in the door. 'Drink,' he said.

Laney eyed the lock on the door. 'Open up,' she said.

'No,' said Tony.

Tony eyed the letter box to see if the bottle would pass but it was too broad around the middle. Instead he shoved the neck of the bottle through the letter box.

'Glass,' said Tony.

Outside the pub Laney lowered her glass to beneath the letter box, and inside the pub Tony tilted the bottle and poured his wife a drink. 'Thanks,' said Laney, taking a big chew on the wine. 'Now this Bill, Tony, who knew this man whose pub was not for sale.'

'I tried to talk to you.'

'We're talking now.'

'You don't know what you've been like, Laney.'

'Speak for your bloody sen,' she said, her accent broadening in her anger, reminding Tony of what she once was, what she still was now.

'Do you remember when we went to Scarborough, Laney?'

'Was Bill there?'

'And we went down on the bank holiday on my motorbike.'

'With Bill in a sidecar.'

'And we ate them fish and chips.'

'The three of us.'

'Sitting out on the headland.'

'And Bill told us how much he'd always wanted to buy a pub, as the old-fashioned Yorkshire sun set on the old-fashioned Yorkshire sea.'

'You're being mean, Laney.'

'I'm livid, you bastard.'

She'd never called him that.

'You should have seen me an hour ago, Tony, when I found bloody out. You'd have been right to keep this door locked.'

Tony had a drink.

'You tried to sell the pub without me, Tony.'

'You'd have had to sign the forms.'

'Under bloody pressure, Tony. Bullying, they call that.'

'Ha!' he said. 'The thought of it. Laney being bullied. They've not built the man strong enough can bully you.'

'Behind my bloody back.'

'Nothing's behind your back, Laney. You see everything and say nothing. Apart from the other night when you finally let on how you feel.'

'Yes,' Laney softened. 'I've been thinking about that.'

'I've thought of nothing else.'

'Come home.'

'Bugger off. All them years you've blamed me and you never had the nerve to tell.'

'I can see why it hurt you. I were wrong in what I said.'

'Wrong! Wrong in what you said!' He jumped up and loomed above her and jabbed his finger down. 'I don't need you telling me wrong from right, telling me who was or wasn't to blame. Don't you think I've made a reckoning of my own?'

He was standing only a foot from her, just the glass between them. His heart was straining at itself, his whole body running a cold sweat.

'*I* can decide.'

He thirsted at the bottle. Part of him was desperate to unbolt the door and walk out and just hold her and cry and get back to normal. But normal was gone now, thrown away. They'd broke the end off normal. Tony looked down. Laney still had her head bowed.

'Go on,' he said, chucking the wine down him. 'Bugger off. You nasty, lying witch. I wish I'd never met you, wish I'd never married you.'

Laney kept still.

'Go on,' said Tony. 'Hop it, you horrible cow.'

He turned and walked off and stood in the dark and watched her. He didn't care what he broke tonight. There was too much love and all of it hurt and he wanted to hurt her most.

When Laney spoke, her voice was shaking. 'You're very rude, Tony Metcalfe.' She stood, 'and if your dear old mum was still with us she'd tan your bloody hide.'

Laney turned and walked away. She looked hunched and cowed. First time, thought Tony, she'd ever looked like a granny. He looked down and stared at the paper, half unfolded on the pub floor, the news from Yorkshire on its old front page. Tattered and dog-eared that paper, stories as dated as Tony's own. He looked up and saw Laney blending now with the darkness far off in the square. It was hopeless. Two old farts in a shitty town in Spain, sniffing round their past like flies round shit. He looked up and saw Laney merge fully into the night.

He'd bust the end off home. He looked at the paper. He hated that bloody thing.

Tony reached down and snatched up the bloody rag. He ripped it in half, then ripped it again, ripping and ripping and ripping the news from home into shreds, ripping it into shreds like his own home had been ripped to shreds. He laughed. He looked down at his birthday present in tatters on the floor. He kicked the newspaper shreds into a pile. He wasn't done yet. He ran to the bar, picked up some napkins, ripped some, chucked them down onto the pile of newspaper. He grabbed the cushion off a nearby chair, chucked it on the pile. He went to the bar, got more napkins, then some more, chucked them on the pile, the matches rattling in his pocket as he moved. He ripped the shirt off his back, the present from Laney, he started to tear at that, rip the stupid shirt into pieces.

He stopped. Tony looked at his half-ripped shirt, at the pile of newspaper and cushion and napkin on the floor. What did he care about Home Sweet Home? Tony pulled matches from his pocket, held them up, opened the box, pulled one out.

Drunk fingers dropped one match and then another. He stared at the pile on the floor, pulled out a third match. This one lit. Tony stepped towards the pile. He placed the burning match to the end of a napkin and watched it start to go, flames growing into the dry paper, the newspaper catching too.

'Tony!' he heard a voice say. 'Open this door.'

JO

What was he doing? The idiot. She'd taken him for many things but she'd not had him down as an arsonist. The flames were burning, his mad face glowing and orange. His eyes were hunting round the pub for more things to burn.

The flames had hold of the napkins now and were licking up the newspaper, reaching out for the birthday shirt, getting a taste for the cushion. He was still looking round.

'Open the door,' Jo said.

What was he doing? He could kill himself.

'You'll get done for arson, Tony, you mad git.'

'Many a muckle makes a buckle or whatever daft shit we say in bloody Yorkshire.'

What was he on about? 'Stop it. Open the door.'

'*Ee by gum*,' Tony said. 'Well I'll go to the top of our stairs.'

He found more napkins. They were stuffed in his trouser pockets. He had another cushion in one hand. He was downing a bottle, wine flooding down his chin. Mild-mannered Tony my arse, thought Jo. He was dancing about like a devil.

She had to stop him.

He lobbed the napkins on the fire, flicked on the cushion. She put her palm on the door, felt the heat of the warmed glass. He took off a shoe. Lobbed that in the fire. He had another swig.

'Stop it, Tony you plank.'

He took off the other shoe. Chucked that on the fire. Chucked on his socks. The flames were licking towards a table now. He saw that himself and dragged the table over, into the fire.

'Stop it.'

Three little bombs sat in her throat, three little words.

His trousers were coming off. She kicked at the bolted door. Kicked and kicked again. The flames were climbing up the table. The glass bowed but the door did not give. She kicked again. The door held again. The glass did not break.

She watched Tony dance, watched his trousers burn. His birthday shirt was hanging out of the fire, the *Yorkshire Evening Post* almost gone. Tony shoved another table forward then tipped it up so a corner was in the fire. She had to do it now. The table was next to the curtains, the curtains led up to the roof.

She had to call out *fire* but she couldn't. Going to Spanish jail for arson was not a good look for a geriatric expat. She had to play the card. She was in the game, she did count. She weighed it all up. What if he couldn't take it? She looked at the fire, looked at him.

'Tony!' He didn't look, didn't stop.

The flames were growing higher.

'Last time, stop.'

It might destroy him but she had to do it. She looked at the flames, took a breath. 'I'm going to tell you the truth, and I'm going to tell you it quickly, and then you're going to let me in, and after that it's up to you what you do. You can tell Laney or you can tell Nick. It's up to you.'

His eyes glowed with flame and drink. She pointed at the fire. 'That is arson. You will go to jail.'

Tony looked at the flames, puzzled, as if seeing them for the first time.

She'd tell him, she had to. 'We'd agreed it the day before that Clare was supposed to come round mine. But when I woke up I was hungry and there was no food in my house and I couldn't wait. Plus the truth was that I wanted to go to yours.

'I knew that Laney was a crabby old mum who preferred a tidy house to a happy kid, but I was ashamed of my house. I knew what was happening at ours was evil... Dad, ashamed of the cuts on his hands. Mum answering the door with sick in her hair.

'I wanted to go to a house where there was food in the cupboards and clean clothes and toothpaste. And yes, Laney didn't even look at me, didn't know my name, but *you* were a sweetheart, from what I'd seen at least, and anyway, I wanted to see Nick.

'Eight-year-olds *can* be in love, Tony, and I'd decided I'd marry Nick. Even though I forgot about that for twenty years until I met him again in London. But Nick didn't look at me, I was just a pest, a friend of his little sister. But I wanted to go to Clare's.

'I walked out the back of our garden and out into the fields.'

Jo looked at Tony. The flames were growing and he was staring into them. She couldn't tell if he was listening or not. She carried on. 'I walked over. High summer flowers and tall, honey grass and just big sky everywhere. I got to the weir and took off my shoes and carried them as I walked across the concrete where the water ran over it thin, just like I always did. Then on the other side I put my shoes back on and I got to the drystone wall at the back of Clare's house.'

The fire was up to the table. Tony just stood and stared.

'I looked down her garden towards the house. I saw you in the kitchen, peeling spuds. A good dad. Not like that slag heap back at mine.

'Sunday lunch,' she said. 'Roast beef and gravy. Yorkshire pud and roast spuds. I didn't know it was Sunday until I got there and saw you. Every day was Friday night round our house.

'Clare came into your back garden. You didn't see her; you were worrying at the lunch. She had a hula hoop that she was chucking about and I called her, loud enough for her to hear but not loud enough for you.'

Tony turned his head to face Jo.

Good, right, keep going.

'Clare looked up and saw me, standing by the wall. She looked back to you, head down in the kitchen, whittling away at the tatties.

She chucked her hoop down and ran across the lawn towards the back wall. She jumped it in one go and as she landed her feet were planted on the grass close to mine, her shoes all shiny and new.'

Jo peered through the glass. He was walking towards Jo now, slowly moving away from the fire towards the door.

'My job,' said Tony. 'I always cleaned her shoes.'

'Saturday nights in front of the TV,' said Jo. 'Clare told me.'

'And this was Sunday, so they'd have been right clean.'

Keep coming Tony.

'Sparkling,' said Jo. 'They were. My shoes were tattered plimsolls, falling apart, my big toe bursting out of one side.'

He was standing now at the other side of the glass.

'We were excited. We didn't know what to do. I forgot I was hungry. There was no school and no grown-ups and the sun was out and the grass was high and chirping.

'We ran through the field and down to the weir and we took off our shoes and Clare jumped up first onto the concrete and before I jumped on I looked down to the bank and saw our shoes, mine all ratty and shit, Clare's all tidy and clean.

'She walked out into the middle and the sun was all on her and the water was laughing as it fell across the weir and she was laughing too, and calling me to come on and play. We played this game where we stood on the weir facing each other and did ballet. We called it ballet. It wasn't ballet, but we called it ballet.'

'But you didn't step out onto the weir.'

'No, I got this feeling, giddy like a cork popping, like a thing inside me that I had no say over.'

'What did you do?'

'I picked one up. One. Good shoes meant a good life and bad shoes meant a bad life. I lifted one of her perfect shoes. Pulled back my arm. Just chucked it at her where she stood on the weir. I was half jealous, half messing. It wasn't hard, just a kid's throw, but enough. She went to dodge it and she fell, her dress falling out behind her as she fell – splash – down into the running water.'

'What did you do?'

'I picked up my own shoes and ran away, laughing. We'd danced so many times on that weir that falling in was just another part of the game. I didn't look back, just ran to the woods, that little copse at the bottom of the field.'

'I know it.'

'I thought she'd be straight after me, sopping and cold and cross, but laughing.'

'But she wasn't,' said Tony.

'She wasn't, no.'

'And you stayed in those trees?'

'Yes, first of all waiting, and then hiding and then when Nick climbed over the garden wall looking for her, I disappeared then. Sloped off back to the drunk house, hid in my room, waited for someone to knock on the door and shout at me and drag me off to some dungeon.'

'But nobody came.'

'Nobody came.'

Tony's hand was flat on the glass of the door. His mouth was held in a horrified circle.

'Open the door, Tony.'

Jo looked at the flames, looked at his white hand pressed on the door.

Tony just stood, white palm pressed against the door like a prisoner trying to touch his family through the jailhouse glass. The connections and feelings and thoughts he'd had for twenty-five years dislodging and tumbling against each other, the words from Jo tumbling through him in an avalanche of feeling, as the flames grew behind.

'But…' said Tony, 'It was my fault.'

'It was me, Tony. Not you. *My* watch.' Three little words like three little bombs. 'I killed Clare.'

His head fell down.

'Open the bloody door.'

*

Later he sat in his bare feet and his pants. The soaked remains of the fire – the burned cushions and shoes and the rest – were in a puddle on the floor. It was dark still, night. Jo was sat beside him shivering.

'You're not with Nick because of this?'

'Some kind of guilt trip marriage you mean? Saving him type-thing?'

Tony nodded.

'I love Nick. When we're together, just me and him... Look, he has his struggles but he will get through. I'm with Nick because of Nick. Far as I know.'

She watched Tony as he looked down sadly at his bare feet.

'Will you tell Nick?' she asked.

'I don't know,' said Tony. 'I feel like a snake trying to digest a bloody lion. I don't know what I'll do. Will *you*?'

She didn't know. What was the calculation here? Was telling the truth more important than saving people pain? 'I don't know either, Tony.'

Jo shifted over and leaned into Tony, resting her head on his shoulder. But Tony pulled away sharply, his body hard and unfriendly. He jumped up, stood above her, a finger jabbing out in an accusing point. 'You killed my girl.'

'I did,' Jo simply said.

'You killed our bloody Clare.'

'I did,' said Jo. 'I'm sorry.'

She watched the rage in his face fall to anguish. 'Why didn't you tell anybody?'

'I was a little scared kid, thought I'd be put in jail. Flogged. Thrown in a well. The adult world was a weird, terrible place to me.'

Tony looked down. 'Why didn't you tell us later?'

'Because I could carry it. I thought I could.'

'We had a right to know. You should have told us.'

'And break your hearts all over again? The dust had settled. I thought it had. Why should everyone swallow the poison when one can live with it alone?'

Tony slumped, his arms at his sides, his face all white and sooty and sad, like the ghost of some long-lost miner.

'I didn't tell anybody, Tony, because I was strong. You can hate me if you like, and I may have been wrong, but what I did I did for love. If you hadn't been such a shit-head you wouldn't know now.'

Tony took the deepest breath. 'How did you live with it?'

Jo shrugged.

'How am *I* supposed to live with it?'

That was the question.

'That's not for me to say,' said Jo. 'I didn't meant to tell you, and I didn't meant to do it.'

Still standing, Tony slowly turned from her and looked out to the square. 'Bet you're glad it's out, Jo.'

Jo said nothing, but yes, yes she was.

The hardest pretending was pretending to yourself, and that was over now. She looked at Tony's back, at his stuck-up hair and his sooty kecks. He was a good man. 'Are you going to tell Laney?' finally she said.

'I don't know,' said Tony, still facing the square. 'I really don't know.'

'What about our buddy movie?'

'I don't know,' said Tony.

TONY

There was a brand new spike in his head.

Tony opened an eye then closed it again. He was alone now. He was curled up under some tablecloths chucked over him for blankets. He tried again with an eye, looked along the floor – his cheek was stuck to a floorboard – to see a mound of wet, half-burned debris.

Next to the mound was a chair on which were placed some fresh clothes, folded up inside a plastic bag. There was a burbling sound above Tony. It was water in the pipes, the shower running in the flat above. He managed to sit up and turn his head and he looked towards the window and beyond it into the village square. It was early, houses still sleeping, their walls looking soft now as butter. The dawn was delicate, barely there.

There was something leaned up against the door outside.

Tony stood up. He walked across the dark pub until he stood at the glass entrance door, grey light turning orange in the square outside. Tony looked at the object that was leaned against the pub door. It was facing the wrong way round but he knew what it was – Pepe's painting, now finished. A gift, as Tony knew, to himself.

He jabbed his hand into his pocket and pulled out the keys. Except his pocket wasn't there. Tony was in his underpants. He looked to the cold fire, saw his semi-burned trousers. He approached, gingerly stuck his hand in a pocket, was relieved to pull out the pub keys. Tony keyed the lock and opened the door and picked up the painting and lifted it inside Home Sweet Home. He relocked the door and walked back towards the bar, placing the painting on a table as he passed. He felt deranged. The immovable new spike in his head was fraught with an awful ache, beyond physical, as though his whole life – his past and his future and everything he had ever felt – had been kicked in the balls by a vicious horse. Tony lay back down under the tablecloths by the doused fire. Improbably he slept, and then it was lighter, and the shower was still running, or else now it was running again.

Nick now stood in the square.

What? Why was Nick there? He was clean and he had combed his hair. His clothes were fresh and they were black. Nick walked in his black clothes straight across the square towards Home Sweet Home. He carried a large, empty bag which he placed down in the same spot that Pepe's painting had been a short time ago.

'Dad!' Nick called into the pub. 'That's the last of the fliers done.'

Tony sat up and looked at his son.

'I just thought Jo's pregnant, you're an old-age pensioner, it's forty bloody degrees.'

Nick was looking at the remains of the fire and shaking his head. He looked disapprovingly to Tony and then back to the fire. He even tutted. 'Jo told me what happened.'

The new spike grated awfully inside him. 'About Clare?'

'About you, blind drunk and mad over Laddo. You do know it's today, don't you?'

'What?'

'His funeral. Come out.'

'No.'

'Did you see the scores, Dad?'

'No.'

'I had a great time in Benidorm.'

'Right.'

'They called me Rocky, the guys from the stag. You've got to come out.'

'No.'

'We knew you'd say that. We are intervening. Me and Mum are.'

'Intervening?'

'Jo has abstained.'

'You've had a family council over Granddad breakdown?'

'Obviously.'

'I go missing for one night... *You've* been missing for weeks.'

Nick smiled. 'I didn't have a campfire in the pub. You've plonked yourself in the middle of the bloody village, Dad. I mean, roll up roll up, come and see the fruitcake.'

'Bad decision.'

'Could have had a quiet mini-break in the hills, got a bit squiffy. Nobody would've known.'

'A spa break.'

'Or a cruise, Dad.'

'Rounding the Cape.'

'That's more of a voyage.'

'I'd prefer a voyage. A cruise seems a bit namby compared to a voyage.'

'A cruise wouldn't satisfy you.'

'Me being so rugged and manly.'

'Come on, Dad, open up. I'll make coffee.'

Tony looked across Nick's shoulder and out into the square. He saw Pepe and Lita dressed smartly, all in black. 'You go across, Nick,' Tony said.

'Come on, Dad,' Nick said, his hand now on the door handle.

'Nick.'

'Come out.'

'Nick,' Tony said. 'Give us a bit.'

Nick let go of the handle. 'You know you're in your pants?'

'I do.'

'See you in a bit,' said Nick. 'Laddo's funeral. Clothes on the chair. Rounding the Horn, yeah?'

'The Cape.'

'Come out, Dad. Mum trusted me to get you out.'

Nick turned and walked across the square towards Pepe and Lita. They were stood outside Pepe's which was open already, presumably for the occasion. A waiter served tots of brandy on the pavement. Pepe and Lita took one each and downed them. Tony felt an itch at his throat. He heard a noise and watched as Jo emerged from the door beside Home Sweet Home. She was in black, Jo, and she was holding Fred in her arms and the lad was in black too. Fred was looking over Jo's shoulder, and he saw Tony plain as day.

'Granddad breakdown,' Fred shouted. 'Granddad episode.'

Jo stopped and turned to Tony and nodded slightly at him once, then turned again and kept on walking towards Pepe's.

Consuela was out onto the square next, with Gabriel and Maria just behind and heading over to Pepe's. Rosa arrived with her family too, also heading to Pepe's, and the drinks were handed out glass by glass by a waiter as each arrived.

Nick was shaking hands. He gave Jo a kiss on the cheek, lifted up his boy and held him. Font and Penny, Claes and Marja, Luis and his wife Marta. They'd all come over, as was the custom, for a strong drink, before taking the short walk down the back of the village to the graveyard. They all came, sadly in ones and twos and threes, until there were only four people missing. Well, three really, Laddo being disqualified.

Then only two were missing when Laney came into the square, with her big shades on and some black linen shawly thing turbaned around her head, like some mad Cleopatra. And then Tony knew there was only one person missing, because he saw that clasping Laney's arm was Shirl. One person missing. Even the widow had got there before Tony.

What a closet. Granddad breakdown.

He stood stinking in his pants on his own in the pub and he watched everyone he loved, more or less, standing together just over in the square.

What sort of bloke was he? Tears were coming off him now. How did he live with this new spike in his head? He looked over the road and saw the mourners. How could Tony go and stand over there?

Tony walked to the chair and picked up the folded-up clothes and put them on. Nick's stuff. Jogging bottoms and a hoody. Tony looked like a teenager. He looked at Pepe's painting. He looked over the square. He had to go. He had to leave his pit. He did not know how to feel these feelings that were raging inside him. He felt that life was at him as sharp as a stiletto and absolutely without mercy. Tony walked towards the glass door. His knees went and he fell and he smashed his face forward against the locked glass so that his face wiped down the glass hard as he fell heavily and smashed to his knees.

Tony knelt on the floor in his pub and cried. Snot smeared from his nose onto his cheeks and lip.

Nick looked over. Tony saw him and quickly stood. Tony swiped his face with a hoody sleeve. Unsteadily, he unlocked the door and stepped out into the square, his knees gone and no good to him, like hinges made of mash potato. He walked in precarious slow motion by the small stone fountain and by the white-washed church and over towards Pepe's.

The group of mourners outside Pepe's was beginning to stir, striking off on the short walk to the graveyard. Shirl, helped by Laney, was at the head; Pepe was at the back, handing the finished glasses to the waiter to take inside. Pepe spotted Tony walking over, and called for a full glass, which he gave to Tony as he arrived.

'Just in time,' said Pepe, slapping Tony on the back.

Tony nearly fell over. He downed his brandy in one gulp. 'Just in time,' he agreed and handed back his glass.

'I got your painting.'

'Do you like it?'

'No.'

'But you will hang it on your wall?'

'No.'

'Can I have it back?'

'No.'

'You're welcome, Tony.'

'Thank you for my painting.'

'You kicked my chair.'

'You stole my buyer.'

'No. You thought my buyer was yours. You were mistaken. You have been mistaken all along.'

Too bloody right he had. Bits of him were burning off every time he breathed.

Tony looked at an olive tree in the graveyard.

Its leaves were darting in the wind and Tony was thinking of being a lad, biking with a pal to a tarn in the next village, laying belly-down on the bank and wafting a jar in the water to try and catch the darting fish.

He thought of the fish as he looked at the olive leaves.

He saw those young fish swim in the water. He saw that the water was clearer than any glass, despite the currents that moved inside it. The purity of the water was the purity of his youth and he felt the purity of age now. Everything was burned off now. The sun was on the water in his youth and the sun was on the leaves in the graveyard and both times were curling up to meet and everything was burned away except the truth.

Laney wouldn't look at Tony. She had one arm round the widow Shirl.

Jo was stood on Laney's other side. Laney was gripping hold of Jo's hand, like she used to do with Clare. Tony saw Jo watching him. She had left him with the choice to tell. Should Tony tell Laney?

Tony looked away. He looked to his son. Nick was holding Fred, jogging the lad up and down, soothing him and whispering. Fred had his finger up his nose, almost to the knuckle. Dying had nothing to do with Fred. It had everything to do with Tony though.

Death felt as close to him as air, close to him as water to a fish. Death was like a coat he was wearing. You could either live with what you knew about life or else you could let it take you under. Tony looked to Jo. Laney clasped her hand like Jo was her own kid, and with that movement, that sure simple gesture of kin, Tony knew that he wasn't telling Laney about Jo and Clare.

It would gut her. Love was a shield to a family. Protection ranked higher than truth. That was the truth. The sun was on Tony's back and the valley was some ship that all of them were sailing in. What was that Laddo had said on the night of Tony's birthday, when they were teasing Tony about home?

...Tony thinks that home is a place, rather than the people you love...

Laddo was going in his grave. Shirl was crying.

Claes was crying too, his face like droopy white dough.

Tony looked round at the folk from the village – the baker's girl, the tobacconist, Raul the mechanic – all the faces that he'd only come to know because he'd been trying to get away.

Then they dropped old Laddo in.

See you, Laddo. See you, mate. Not so clumsy now.

He caught Laney's eye but she looked away.

God it was gloomy, not very Laddo.

Tony pulled his phone out. He wouldn't have done last year, he'd have just grumbled through it, tried to please. But he knew that Shirl never put her phone on silent, and he guessed that wouldn't have changed, even today. He sent her a text.

Bit moody this, he wrote. *Can I liven it up for Laddo?*

Shirl had some flirty whistle as her ringer. The priest glared but you couldn't bollock the widow, could you? Shirl rummaged round in her pocket and read the message. She smiled and lifted her head and looked round for Tony and nodded. Tony coughed and stepped forward.

'Do you mind?' Tony said to the priest. 'Have you finished your sayings?'

The priest nodded and people stayed quiet, which meant Tony carried on.

'I was mates with Laddo, so Shirl's just told me I can, er. Well.'

He coughed.

'Now my mate Laddo had three main passions. Number one, Shirl, of course, standing here so magnificently. Two, getting pissed... Sorry. Drunk. Which we are going to do in a bit. And three, football. He also liked it when his mates looked like idiots. So what we're going to do, to honour our fallen comrade, is chuck that together and sing the theme tune from *Match of the Day*.'

'Which one?' asked Claes. 'There have been a number of versions.'

'The theme tune we all know,' said Tony. 'The famous one.'

Tony appealed to Nick, who shrugged. Laney gave him the idiot face.

'The well-known one.'

Tony eyed Rosa and Maria, who looked confused. Nobody seemed to know it.

'We could do *The Dam Busters*,' suggested Shirl. 'Laddo loved war films.'

'Perfect,' said Tony. He started humming but nobody joined in with him. Tony fell silent. 'Any other ideas?' he asked.

'*Waterloo* by Abba,' Marja shouted. 'Let's have a disco!'

'Disco!' shouted Fred.

'Prog rock,' said Luis, holding his bandana. 'Is very overlooked as a genre.'

'I'd agree with that,' said Nick.

'Christ,' said Jo.

'Hey!' objected the priest.

'*They all want me, they can't have me, hey Macarena*,' sang Chico.

'Whale music,' said Lita.

'Bebop,' said Pepe.

'Really!' said Nick. 'You like that?'

'Christ,' said Jo.

'Pub,' said the priest.

Tony pulled on the door to Home Sweet Home, wedged it open then stepped inside, running his hand down the switches to turn on every light. He knew what to do. 'On the house, everything,' Tony said. 'Luis, *haz todo lo posible*.'

Luis smiled and headed off to the kitchen to get stuck in.

Nick bombed out the back and got the bin, started clearing up the fire. Tony took some empty bottles off the table. He picked up

Pepe's painting and hung it on the wall. Tony went behind the bar and started getting glasses out as he watched the mourners troop inside. He intended to host a fearsome wake. He had other plans besides. Tony watched Nick as he chucked the charred paper and shoes and cushions into the bin.

Jo was stood in the doorway, not coming in. He went towards her.

'Morning,' said Tony, bashful suddenly.

'Morning,' Jo said, looking over Tony's shoulder to Nick.

'I've not told them,' said Tony. 'In case you were wondering.'

'I was wondering.'

'What about you?'

'I don't know Tony. Maybe I need to tell Nick at least. But not today.'

'No, not today. How do you feel, Jo?'

'About ten thousand stone lighter since telling you.'

'Good,' he said.

'Want a hand serving?' Jo said, coming round the bar.

Tony nodded and smiled. He picked up a bottle. 'Rosé!' he called, looking round for Shirl. 'Shirl knows why.'

'Your birthday,' Shirl piped up from a chair by the window. 'Laddo chucked it all over you.'

'He did.' Tony stood up on a chair and addressed the room. 'This lady here,' he gestured towards Shirl by the window. 'Make room for her, give her a bit of air, this lady here is the goddess behind Laddo's throne.'

'The what?' said Font.

'Exactly. And in her honour, everything all day is free. We will feast as lords and we will knock things over and we will wear our wonky glasses.'

'To Laddo.' Tony pointed his glass to Shirl.

'To Laddo,' Shirl replied, crying.

They chucked the wine back.

'Not that he wasn't a bit, you know,' said Shirl.

'What?' two or three people said.

'Sweaty? Heavy-set?' said Pen.

Somebody shushed her. Everyone was waiting to hear what Shirl would reveal. 'Well he was very peculiar about food.'

'He was,' said Tony. 'Very fussy about pastries.'

'And relish. We had seven or eight relishes open in the fridge.'

'And despite never fishing,' explained Tony for the benefit of those unacquainted with the foibles of Laddo, 'he subscribed to an angling magazine.'

'His mate ran it,' Shirl explained. 'Carl with the ankles. Got very bad towards the end.'

And then from the stage came a sound, a trumpet, and when Tony looked he saw Maria was up there, having a parp, wanting to play, and Maria looked at Shirl, sort of to see if it was okay, and Shirl nodded and Maria smiled back and then Maria had another parp on her trumpet and Rosa stepped towards the stage herself, carrying an instrument case which she then opened.

Tony looked around. Shirl was doing okay, but where was Nick? None of this worked without Nick. Tony walked to the stage.

'You two,' he said in Spanish. 'Call your mates, get the band down, would you?'

Rosa and Maria smiled and got on their phones. Tony looked around and spotted something out of the window. Cars were arriving in the square. expat cars he'd never seen before. Where was bloody Nick? Tony looked around. Then there was Laney, coming in from the kitchen, and *she* was talking to Nick. There they were together. Tony walked over, addressing Laney first.

'Sorry, Laney, about the Bill thing.'

'What?'

'I should have found a way to say it.'

'Okay,' said Laney. 'You're sorry about the Bill thing.'

'Yes. I am.'

'I'll leave you two to talk,' said Nick.

'No, Nick.' Tony grabbed Nick's arm. 'I need some advice on the, er...'

Nick looked to Laney. They exchanged a *fruitcake* look.

'I need some advice on the lighting,' Tony said.

Nick looked above the stage. 'There is no lighting.'

'I need some help with the...' Tony dragged Nick across the pub, spotting new faces amongst the wake, more expat cars arriving in the square. 'Your fliers have done the job, Nick.'

'Oh Christ,' said Nick, looking round. 'Really? Shall I go round and tell people we're closed?'

'No, no,' said Tony. 'More the merrier.' Tony stopped walking. 'Will you play, Nick?'

Tony pointed towards the stage and the battered old piano, now buffed up.

'Shirl can't play,' said Tony. 'Have to be you.'

'What? Me? No.'

'You have to do it.'

'Dad.'

'It's the only way.'

'What?'

'Clare said.'

'Piss off, Dad.'

'Clare told me that you should play.'

'She came to you in a dream?'

'More or less.'

'This is a story from your voyage around the Cape?'

'It is. Clare said if you played that Laney would dance.'

'She never said that.'

'She did, Nick. She said that.'

'Do you believe that?'

'Nothing else works.'

'Nor will this.'

'We'll never find out, will we Nick, unless you play?'

Friends of Maria and Rosa came through the door with more trumpets, a tuba, a slide trombone. Nick watched them tumble in and head towards the stage. Tony saw Nick look over to Laney.

'Mum will never dance with you.'

'She will.'

'She always says no.'

'She'll not this time.'

'How come?'

'She'll not say no because I'm not going to ask her.'

'What?'

'I'm not going to ask her.'

'What?'

'She's going to ask me.'

'Bollocks.'

'We'll never know, will we Nick,' said Tony, staring at the piano.

'Clare said this?'

'In a dream.'

Nick exhaled.

'Go on,' said Tony, putting his hand out.

Nick's hand was shaking. Tony took his drink.

'Go on,' Tony repeated. 'Get it done. Get it over.'

Nick nodded. He walked towards the stage and climbed up alongside the village band, who were still parping and honking and getting ready. Nick pulled out the piano stool, which was far too small, and sat down. Tony looked across the pub to Laney, who hadn't noticed Nick as yet, and then, '*Row row, row your boat,*' Nick started to play, '*Gently down the stream.*' And Laney was looking to the stage now, seeing her Nick at the piano, which she'd never done in years, and playing that song as well, that rhyme.

'*Merrily, merrily, merrily.*'

Laney was looking over to Tony. He knew what she was thinking. About that day in summer, not late, all those years ago with Tony coming home in his biffed-up car and bolting down the hall to join in with his family, then little Clare tugging closed the curtains to hide her mum and let her mum and dad dance. He knew Laney was thinking it. He knew she was.

Nick knew it too, he must have done, because Nick now played a waltz, and Laney put her drink down. She turned around and walked away from the music then she stood still and turned back round, walking slowly across the crowded pub towards Tony.

'I know that I'm a shit-house,' Laney said when finally she got there, 'and I'm slow to cotton on.'

Tony stayed quiet. Nick kept on playing. The wake thronged around.

'And you're right, I'm not ill,' said Laney. 'Or else I'm depressed if I am.'

'You look pretty.'

'Can we dance?'

'There's a big crowd in, Laney,' said Tony, glancing about.

'Never mind,' said Laney. 'I'll shut the curtains.' She took his hand and held Tony and started to move with him, her head on his shoulder. 'Remember the first time?' asked Laney.

'Dancing in a cleaning cupboard. Living the high life.'

'We had chips as well. Would love some bloody chips now.'

'An Eccles cake.'

'A piece of haddock.'

'Roasties and gravy.'

'Floury bap with chips.'

'We're back to the chips. Chip butty. Rather have a naan bread.'

'Naan bread butty? You're mad. You've changed.'

She smiled, sighed. 'I never tell you anything.'

'Nope.'

'Just sweep it under the rug.'

'But your rug is getting lumpy.'

'My rug is in the air.'

'And what's underneath it?'

'Well, treasures, now I've had a clear-out…'

'Are you sure you've had a clear-out, Laney?'

Laney moved closer. 'There's a place I want to take you in the woods.'

'Will I need protecting?'

'There's a pile of stones I made.'

'Okay,' Tony said.

'I look at that photo you keep of her.'

He was determined that Laney would say it. He couldn't trust this unless she did.

'This photo,' asked Tony, 'is it under your rug?'

'Not anymore.' Laney pulled the photo from her pocket. 'It's in my hand.'

'Right.'

'I miss our Clare,' said Laney. 'I miss you, Tony, and I miss our Clare.'

'I miss Clare too.'

'I will move back to England with you, Tony.'

'I don't want to. I tried to get away but home is here now.'

'We'll visit then,' said Laney, kissing his neck.

The brass joined in with Nick now and Laney was holding Tony, the kids from the village cobbling together a ragged friendly waltz. *Oom cha cha*, danced Tony and Laney, round and round and round.

A crowd stood in the village square. They were looking at the mayor, sleepy Gabriel, staring at the scissors he held in his hands. Gabriel passed the scissors to Shirl, who took them then cut the ribbon which was tied around the handle of the new engraved tap.

Laddo Atkinson Memorial Tap, it read.

Tony looked up to the church tower.

Forever in the Shadow of The Nip.

The crowd clapped as the ribbon parted. Shirl turned the handle. Water now ran from the once-dry tap. Tony smiled.

Sleepy Gabriel smiled too. He reached into his pocket and pulled out a curled-up piece of paper which he handed to Tony. '*Residencia permanente*,' Gabriel said.

Tony took the papers and thanked Gabriel, who'd used his political influence to push the Metcalfes' papers through, now they were a real part of the valley. The Metcalfes were staying on for good.

Tony looked over to Pepe's. Except it wasn't Pepe's now. It was Bill's. Tony saw Bill standing alone outside his empty bar.

The crowd followed Gabriel and Shirl across to Home Sweet Home for the celebration drinks. Tony watched them flow into his pub, Laney holding court behind the bar. Tony looked back to the lonely figure of Bill. He walked across the square towards him.

'Come and join us, Bill,' he said. 'Please.'

JO

It was cold being back in London. There was an extra blanket on the bed. Jo lay awake in the night. Fred was asleep in the bedroom next door. The new son Chico was sleeping too, in a Moses basket at the foot of their bed. Their tiny London flat felt full but peaceful.

Jo was decided. She had to do it. It was up to Tony if he told Laney or not – he was the judge of that – but it was up to her to tell Nick.

She was – what was the phrase of Tony's? – shitting chutney.

Jo climbed from the bed and walked over to Nick's chest of drawers and slowly opened the top drawer and carefully snaked her hand right in to the back, where she knew that he kept it.

She pulled out Clare's small, polished shoe. Jo took the shoe and went back to bed and turned her bedside light on and lay down and propped herself up by her elbow.

Nick was sleeping on his side, facing towards her. She put the shoe down on the mattress between them. 'Nick,' she gently called. 'Nick.'

He stirred, opened one eye, fixed it on the shoe.

Nick jammed his eye closed.

'Nick,' Jo said.

He coughed. 'Really?' he said.

'Yes,' said Jo.

Nick exhaled. 'Really?' he said again.

'Yes.'

'Okay.' He rolled onto his back, eyes still closed, voice slow.
'Nick...'

'Jo, wait. I sussed it out myself since we got back.'

'What?'

'Running down to the weir that day I saw some kid just playing,
I thought, in the trees, but I just ran to my sister. Could have been
any kid.'

'But it wasn't any kid,' said Jo.

Nick paused, kept his eyes closed. 'And then all that in Spain...'

Jo waited but he said no more. She kept very still. After a long
time she said, 'And what about us?'

'Oh Christ God, I'm fucked if I know, kids will be up in an hour,
can we just get some sleep, I've got so much shit to do.'

'But, Nick?'

Silence.

'Nick?'

He opened one eye and he looked at her kindly. 'Shush, baby,'
Nick said. 'We're good.'

Then he rolled on his side and slept.

Jo drove the bust-up family car south through London, the dual
carriageway giving way to suburban streets. The car heater was
broken, the windscreen steamed up. She could see bugger all. Jo
glanced to Tony in the passenger seat. She hadn't brought the kids.
Nick and Laney were babysitting back at the flat. Peas in a pod,
mother and son these days.

Jo was driving Tony over to see her brother Will. Tony and Will
had spoken three weeks ago at the hospital when Chico was born,
and Jo had seen then that the men needed to meet again.

Of course they did. The two had something in common.

They both knew about her and Clare.

Jo knew now that she hadn't only gone to Spain for Nick and his
family. She had summoned it all on her own head.

Jo turned the car left, roads getting thinner and thinner, each one less suitable for turning back. What Jo had confessed to Tony in the pub, might she not have doused his fire with some other words instead?

Had telling Tony the truth been the only way?

Of course not. But the guilty always want to confess, explain themselves. You just had to watch people to know their truth, they'd cough it all up eventually. Jo had wanted to tell Tony.

She stopped the car, put the handbreak on. She looked at her brother's house. She was glad that Tony wasn't asking her to go in with him while he spoke with Will. It would be too rough in there for her, two men talking about what she had done.

She would feel like a specimen and a problem. She would feel like a case.

'I'm scared,' Tony said.

'What of?' asked Jo.

'Of talking to your brother about you, about Clare.'

'It's a bit messed up,' said Jo. 'Thanks for not…'

'…Reporting you for murder. You chucked a shoe. The unluckiest person in the world.'

Jo looked away.

'I trust you,' said Tony. 'Weirdly. And now you are going to trust me.'

'What?'

The fire and the funeral were the last burn for Tony, but for Jo the last burn was now.

'You're coming in.'

'No.'

'I only said you weren't to get you to come,' Tony said. 'You're going to come in.'

'I'm not.' Nobody could make her.

'I trust you, now you trust me.'

She sighed, deflated, her head collapsed onto the steering wheel. 'What do you want?'

'Just sit there and listen. I need you. You being there will make it more real.'

She could see that. There was no way out. Jo nodded.

She climbed out of the car. Tony climbed out too and he met her on the pavement. Arm-in-arm they walked up to the red-brick semi. A small passageway led down to the side, a gatepost at the front of the passageway had a small plaque screwed to it: *Will Dobson, Designer*.

They couldn't walk down the thin passageway side-by-side, so they straggled down, Jo first holding Tony's hand behind. They came out into a small back garden. Jo pointed down towards the trees which they approached then passed under to see a long, low building running the width of the garden.

Lights glowed inside, a drawing board was angled up by a window, the door was slightly ajar. Jo hesitated then stepped inside, kicked off her shoes on the mat, peeled off her coat. Tony did the same, closing the door behind him.

Will was at a drawing board with his back to them. He heard them and turned and smiled and walked straight over. 'Jo,' he said with a kiss and a smile.

She absolutely loved her brother. When she'd gone under he had pulled her out. Though who was pulling him out she'd never quite fathomed.

'Have any trouble,' Will asked Tony, 'getting her in from the kerb?'

'A bit,' said Tony. 'But it was never in any serious doubt.'

'You two,' said Jo.

'Tea?' her brother asked. 'Sit down, Tony.'

Will gestured towards the little rattan sofas near the small wood-burning stove.

Tony sat down on the sofa and Jo took the chair as Will stepped over towards the kettle.

'I put something out for you, Tony, on the coffee table.'

Jo looked down to the small table and saw three photographs placed in a small pile. Tony reached forward and picked them up. Jo watched Tony lean back on the sofa.

'The first photograph is our parents, the drunk and the villain.' Will had his back to them, rummaging round a cupboard for tea. 'I've got no tea, truth be told,' he said. 'I drink more coffee.'

234

'Coffee's better,' said Tony. 'Wine is better than that.'

'Of course,' said Will, shutting the cupboard and hitching a bottle from the shelf.

Jo watched Tony as he looked at the picture of her first parents. She knew exactly the photo he was looking at.

'Lovely to look at,' said Will, 'but a nightmare to rely on.'

Will pulled up a chair and joined them by the stove. He laid out three glasses and started opening the wine. 'Drink for you sis yeah, now you've sprogged.'

'A little one,' said Jo.

Will gave her a wink, looked over to Tony. 'They were very good at arguments...'

'But they weren't too good at love,' said Jo.

'No,' Will agreed. 'They weren't too good at that.'

Will passed the wine glasses to Tony and Jo, then reached over and took Jo's free hand.

'That next photo,' Will said, 'is Auntie Joan.'

Jo felt Will squeeze her hand. 'It was much harder for Jo when Joan took us from Mum and Dad. I was a teenager, and I didn't live there long.'

'She looks very nice,' said Tony, eyeing the photo. 'Love her smile.'

'Then you came here to live with me, didn't you?'

Jo nodded.

'Did about ten degrees, helped me with my kids.'

'Oh Christ!' Tony said.

He had found it, Jo knew. She couldn't see what Tony was seeing, but she knew exactly what it was. The photo of her and Clare together. The only one.

'I took that,' said Will.

Tony looked at the photo and Jo looked at Tony. She knew what he was seeing: Clare's face, white as smoke next to Jo's white own. Tony covered his eyes. Jo couldn't take it. This was her final burn.

Will squeezed her hand. Tony looked up from the photo and looked right at her. Tears streamed down his cheeks.

'I'll be your dad if you'll have me, Jo.'

ACKNOWLEDGEMENTS

The book is set in Parcent, in the Pop Valley, Marina Alta, a village the Spanish writer Gabriel Miró called 'a paradise between the mountains'. My parents lived there as expats from 1998 to 2013 and I visited often, first alone, then with my wife, then with my own family.

The valley, the expat way of life there, suggested Paul Scott's 1977 novel, from which my work takes its title, but Scott wrote of a repressed colonial set, whereas the *Costas* boast ribald people. So I used Roddy Doyle's *Barrytown Trilogy* – particularly *The Van* – as inspiration for writing with warmth about working people. Roddy Doyle, Paul Scott, killer writers – thank you both.

I was told by men with expensive educations that people don't want to read about the working classes. I'd like to thank these men for the motivation.

The first draft of this book was read by Ali Eastwood and by Paul Lenz and Andrew Chapman and Susie Jones. Firm friends all. Thank you.

David Haviland at the Andrew Lownie Literary Agency believed in this book from the first time he read it. Thank you, David.

Matt Casbourne at Duckworth understood this book and backed it. Thank you, Matt. Thanks also to Duckworth's Thogdin Ripley, David Marshall and Danny Lyle. The cover by David Wardle is right in the slot.

The process of writing this book was documented by the British Library in a unique keystroke capture project. Thanks to Nora

McGregor, Jeremy Leighton John, Jonathan Pledge, Rachel Foss and Stella Wisdom, for your work along the way.

Working with my screenwriting partner Jeremy Sheldon has made me a better writer. Thanks, Jerry.

Thanks to my colleagues and friends at Oxford International Centre for Publishing Studies – Leander Reeves, Adrian Bullock, Angus Phillips, and not least Sarah Franklin, who encouraged me on an early draft.

Brother Lee makes hard times less hard. Thank you.

Big love and massive farts to Mabel and Bessie.

Anna, habibi, thank you.

My Dad, Geoff, was best man on my wedding day, and he's best man again today.

Craig Taylor lives in Oxford, teaching at the Oxford International Centre for Publishing Studies where he is an Associate Lecturer. He also teaches for Jericho Writers and is a freelance editor of fiction. Under the pen name C. M. Taylor, he is the author of *Premiership Psycho* (Corsair 2011) and *Group of Death* (Corsair 2012), two-thirds of a satirical trilogy. *Premiership Psycho* has been optioned for television.